TRAPHOUSE KING 2
Levels To The Game
HOOD RICH

I0566109

Lock Down Publications and Ca$h Presents TrapHouse King A Novel by Hood Rich

TrapHouse King 2

Lock Down Publications
P.O. Box 870494
Mesquite, Tx 75187

Visit our website:
www.lockdownpublications.com

First Edition July 2018
Printed in the United States of America

Lock Down Publications
Like our page on Facebook: Lock Down Publications @
www.facebook.com/lockdownpublications.ldp

Cover design and layout by: **Dynasty CoverMe**
Book interior design by: **Shawn Walker**
Edited by: **Lashonda Johnson**

TrapHouse King 2

Stay Connected with Us!

Text **LOCKDOWN** to 22828 to stay up-to-date with new releases, sneak peeks, contests and more...

Submission Guidelines:

Submit the first three chapters of your completed manuscriptto:ldpsubmissions@gmail.com,

Subject line: Your book's title.

The manuscript must be in a .doc file and sent as an attachment. The document should be in Times New Roman, double-spaced and in size 12 font. Also, provide your synopsis and full contact information. If sending multiple submissions, they must each be in a separate email.

Have a story but no way to send it electronically? You can still submit to LDP/Ca$h Presents. Send in the first three chapters, written or typed, of your completed manuscript to:

LDP: Submissions Dept
Po Box 870494
Mesquite, Tx 75187

DO NOT send original manuscript. Must be a duplicate.

Provide your synopsis and a cover letter containing your full contact information.

Thanks for considering LDP and Ca$h Presents.

Hood Rich

Chapter 1

I took a deep breath and a minor step back, raised my foot, then kicked in the Vic's master bedroom door so hard that it caused it to crash inward with a loud boom, leaving it hanging part way from the hinges. The impact made me stumble. I nearly fell on my ass as Paper ran past me and into the room with his pistol out. There was a loud scream from inside as I gathered myself.

"Everybody lay the fuck down! This is the one and only time I'mma say it!" Paper hollered, rushing toward the bed where the couple was scrambling to cover themselves and follow his directives.

Paper was my right-hand man. Had been ever since the fourth grade. He was the only man that I trusted in this world. We hustled together, hit licks together, and side by side on multiple occasion we'd bussed our guns together.

After I regained my footing, I ran in behind him, ready to go into action. This lick was sure to bring us a minimum of twenty kilos of dope, and I wasn't entirely sure how much money though I was expecting a lot because that's what Aaliyah, my female companion, had told me to expect. In fact, it was her that had put the whole lick together in the first place. We were operating under the banner of one hand washing the other. She'd put this lick together for me, and if it was a success, then I was to handle some deadly business for her. It was the life we lived.

I ran behind Paper and nearly bumped into him. Then, I stopped and looked over his shoulder. For the first time I was able to get a good look at the vic that we were there to hit. I identified him immediately. When I did, I felt my heart skip a beat. My heart dropped into my stomach and I felt like I could no longer breathe as I watched Paper grab him by the neck before slapping him across the face with the pistol, causing his blood to skeet across the head board.

He flew backward as Paper grabbed him again and jammed his pistol into his forehead, cocking the hammer.

Aaliyah jumped out of the bed, dressed in a short, red see-through night gown and slid her hand underneath the mattress to come up with a key. "Y'all gotta kill him, or we're all fucked. It ain't gon' matter because I got the key to his safe, so we're good." She ran around the bed and over to me and got ready to kiss me on the cheek.

I stood frozen in place, unable to move by the sights of the vic.

Paper grabbed a big pillow and placed it over his face before putting the barrel of his gun against it; I imagined ready to blow his brains all over the mattress while he laid there barely moving, weak from the attack. "Say yo' prayers, white man." He growled through clenched teeth.

That's when I snapped out of my zone and ran toward the bed with haste. "Bruh, wait, don't kill him! That's my father!" I hollered, jumping on to the bed and pulling on Paper's shoulder.

Paper's eyes bugged out of his head. "What?" He looked back at me with a confused look on his face.

I moved him off my old man and pulled my father up by his white t-shirt. "Pop? Pop, you good?" I asked.

Blood gushed out of the crack in his head. His face was red, and he had his eyes closed. He looked ten years older than he did the last time I'd seen him. He slowly opened his eyes. "Rich? Rich? Is that you, son?" He groaned before putting two fingers up to his forehead.

I pulled my mask off and nodded. "Yeah, Pop. What the fuck are you doing in Milwaukee?"

He groaned in pain again, squeezing his eyelids together. "I've been back and forth from here to New York for the last year. I couldn't stay away from your mother, son. I'm so sorry that she's gone. I wish I could have saved her." He sat up and scooted backward until his back was against the headboard. "What's all this?" He looked from me to Paper, then over to Aaliyah who looked like she was about to freak out.

She shook her head. "N'all, fuck that. You mean to tell me that this white dude is your father, Rich? So, what does that mean for me? Huh?" She whimpered, biting on one of her fingers.

I slid off the bed and put my pistol into the small of my back. "Don't worry, Aaliyah, you're straight. Ain't none of this shit about to leave this room. Ain't that right, Pops?"

My old man nodded, took the sheet and dabbed his bloody forehead with it. "What is this, Rich?" he asked again, wincing in pain.

I blew air through my teeth. "This what I gotta do to survive ever since you left our family to fend for ourselves. Had moms injecting that poison into her arms. Left my sisters without a father. All for what? So, you could go off and raise your Italian family and say screw us? Just act like we never existed? Huh?"

My father was a full-blooded Sicilian. He'd came over from Sicily a few years before I was born, and he and my mother fell in love. Prior to meeting him, she had been a flight attendant, and I guessed they'd flirted back and forth on numerous occasions until they fell for one another. Unbeknownst to my mother, my father was plugged into the Bertolli Mafia, which was the third strongest crime family in the United States of America, behind the Gambino's. Well, after my father fell in love with my mother, he started to catch heat from those of his crime family. There was a golden rule that said that no made man could be involved with any woman that wasn't Italian, and any woman that was of color was extremely forbidden.

My father was warned time and time again to stop messing with my mother or he would never become a made man. But, he was just as crazy about her as she was him, so they took to sleeping around in the shadows. Long story short, by the time Kesha was born, my father was in too deep with the mob and was given an ultimatum: leave his family of niggers behind or meet his maker. He chose to leave us behind and go on with his life. But before he did, he got my mother hooked on heroin and would supply her the drugs for free until he cut all ties with the family altogether.

My father swallowed and groaned in pain. "I didn't have a choice, son. If I didn't leave you guys behind, the Bertolli family was going to kill me and all of you guys just to make a statement to the other brothers and women of the family. I couldn't allow for that to happen, so I had to keep my distance."

Paper shook his head. "What!" He paced with his gun along his temple. Then he extended it and pointed it at my father. "Look, I don't give a fuck who this white man is to you, Rich. We came to get this money and dope, and I ain't leaving without that shit. So, what's up?" he asked, looking over at me with wild eyes.

Aaliyah exhaled and wiped her mouth with a hand. "Rich, he gotta go. Dude plugged with the mob and shit. You know he gon' kill us. You might be straight, but we ain't." She came over and stood beside Paper.

My father smiled and tilted his chin upward, pointing to the soft groove under it. "You wanna kill me, kid? Huh. You gonna let him do this shit to me, son? Let him kill your old man? You hate me that much?" He snarled.

Paper kneeled on the bed and slammed the gun's barrel directly to the spot that my father was pointing to. "Rich, what's the word? You know how I get down, bruh. I can't be looking over my shoulder for no mob. Tell me what's good. Am I blowing his brains out or not?"

"Please, Rich. Please, let him kill him. I know Paul. He's going to come for me and him. He might let you live, but he will never accept my betrayal lying down. We're as good as dead," Aaliyah said still biting on her finger nail.

"What's good, Rich?" Paper hollered.

My father looked me over with his head tilted backward. Blood ran down his forehead and onto his neck before dripping on the white sheets. "It's your call, Rich. If this is the way you want me to go out, I'll accept it. I deserve this fate. I've killed countless men." He swallowed.

"What's good, Rich?" Paper growled through clenched teeth. "Let's get this money, my nigga."

"Let him do it, Rich," Aaliyah honed in. "We can get everything and move on with our lives. I told you I had you, and I do. Why should we switch up the game plan?"

My mind was spinning a million miles an hour. There was my father, my flesh and blood. The man that had given me life, and in sense had taken life away from me. Our family had been through hell and back ever since we'd left New York. We'd experienced so much pain that we all were a little broken inside.

"What's the word son?" my father asked as a puddle of blood formed on the sheet beside him.

Paper forced the gun further into his skin. "Let me blow his head off, bruh. We're all the family that we got. It's been like that since the fourth grade."

I saw a vision of my mother lying on our living room floor, foaming at the mouth, shaking as if she was having a seizure, dying a violent death by overdose because of the drugs that I had given her. I had been the cause of my mother's untimely death, and in that moment, I knew that I couldn't stand by and watch my father be killed as well. Especially knowing that I could prevent it. I would have never been able to live with myself, no matter how much he'd hurt our family.

I shook my head. "N'all. Leave him alone, bruh. I can't let you do that." I said, looking my pops in the eyes.

Paper lowered the gun and swung it at the air. "Fuck! Man, this some bullshit. Now how we supposed to get paid?"

Aaliyah put her hands over her face. "This isn't happening. This can't be happening." She took them away and walked to the bed. "Promise him, Paul. Promise him that you won't kill me or him over there for doing this shit to you. Promise him right now on you guys' blood," she demanded.

My father dabbed at the blood leaking out of his skull, then looked me in the eyes. "Son, you have my word that I will not lay a hand on them. I understand that this was just business. It was nothing personal." He swallowed then smiled weakly.

Paper shook his head. "We making a mistake, bruh. I feel it. Ain't no way I would accept this shit from nobody— son or not. I'd whack his lil' ass on the strength. I say we handle this business and get this bread. You know, stick to the game plan like ol' girl was saying."

"*Aaliyah.*" Aaliyah corrected him.

"Yeah, stick to the game plan like *Aaliyah* was saying."

I was about to say what I was really feeling when my father interrupted me. "If it's money that you want, I can take care of that for you with no problem. The same goes for the dope. I won't allow for this to be a loss on either end. Like I said, I understand it's just business and nothing personal."

Paper nodded. "Yeah, well just how much money and dope are you talking about, old man? Because had we hit yo' ass up we'd a been well off. I'm trying to be set for a minute, so we can hit these slums the way we're supposed to. And it wouldn't have bothered me one bit if it was blood money." He sucked his teeth.

Aaliyah shook her head. "This shit cannot end well. I'm screwed. I done went from one lunatic pimp looking for me, to a whole ass mafia family. Fuck. I trusted you, Rich. Had I known we were about to go this route, I would have never fucked off Paul." She lowered her head and sat on the chair that was across from the bed, next to the window.

"Yo, you good, Aaliyah. Just chill, ma. I ain't gon' let nothing happen to you, and our deal is still valid. In my opinion, you've held up your end of things." I walked over to her and wrapped my arm around her shoulders. "You got my word on that, ma, okay?"

She nodded, looking into my eyes, and as usual causing me to feel some type of way. I didn't care that she'd sold pussy before. Whenever She and I were in the same room there was always something in the air— a feeling that bounced back and forth from her to me, and vice versa.

Paper waved us off. "What's good, Paul?"

My father sat up further. "Aaliyah, you have the key to my safe. I want you to use it. In the safe you'll find thirty kilos of pure Colombian cocaine, and three hundred thousand dollars. You guys can take it. Before you do, Rich, I'm going to need you to fuck me up and shoot me here three times," he said, pointing to a spot between his chest and stomach. "But not with those Glocks. I want you to use the gun in my nightstand. It's a forty-five automatic with a silencer. The same guns used by the Mexican Cartel that I was supposed to be closing the deal with. We need for the Bertolli family to think that I was robbed and betrayed by those bastards, that way we can wage a war and take over their drug territories down in Chicago, Gary and Detroit. It's extremely important. Don Bertolli has become too familiar with the cartel, so much so, that he's begun to squeeze some of his own out. I'm third in line to receive his throne. If I can show that he's starting to make a lot of wrong moves that hurt the family, I can have him ousted and I can move up a slot before I make my final move to become the Don in my own right."

Paper walked around to the nightstand and pulled open the drawer, finding the forty-five and cocking it back. "Yo, I'll pop him up if you want me to. Let's get this show on the road. We ain't got all day," he said, standing over my father, extending the gun so that he was aiming it at his chest.

My old man curled his upper lip. "You idiot. Does it look like I have my bullet proof vest on?" he snapped.

I tapped Paper on the shoulder. When he turned around to look at me, I took the gun out of his hand. "I got this, bruh. Pop, where is your vest? We need to put a shirt on you or something." I stepped closer to the bed, looking into his hazel eyes. His wavy hair

19

was all over the place. Blood continued to come out of his wound, running down the side of his face.

Five minutes later, I straddled my father with my fist balled up.

"Go ahead, son. Make sure you work me over pretty good. Make it look believable. Then, I need for you guys to trash the place and get as far away from here as possible. I'll be in touch."

I nodded and raised my fist.

Paper came back into the room with two duffle bags. "Yo, this old nigga was holding, Rich. I swear its good-good. Handle yo' business and meet me in the car. I'm out, kid. Come on, Aaliyah."

She walked past me, stopped and kissed my cheek. "Hurry up, baby. Ain't no telling whose watching this house, especially since he's deeply plugged into the mob." She rubbed my chest, then hurried behind Paper.

I could hear their footsteps pounding down the stairs, making their retreat. I took a deep breath and looked down on my father, preparing to do some damage to his face. "Aight, here we go, old man." I raised my fist high into the air and was ready to bring it down when my father stopped me.

"Wait, Rich. Before you do it, tell me, how are the girls? Do they remember me?" He blinked and scratched the collar around his shirt.

I nodded. "Yeah, they remember you. Everybody remember you, Pop. It's a shame you didn't remember us!" I brought my fist down at full speed, crashing it into his jaw, doing the same with my left one, and then the right one was crashing into his face again.

I allowed myself to black out. I thought back to the days when my father would slap my mother around in front of me as if it was the most natural thing in the world. Beating her until she wound up on the floor, curled into a ball, trying her best to protect herself before I ran in to help her. Back

then I was so small that one hit from my father would often knock me out cold. In those days, I hated his guts. I hated him because he was nothing more than a bully, ashamed of us because of our color. *Wham. Wham. Wham. Wham. Wham.*

My fists were unforgiving as they smashed into his cheeks until his face was swollen and pink. I got off the bed and extended my gun. "Despite all the heartache and pain you've caused this family, I still love you, old man. Never forget that."

He sat up further in the bed, struggling to breathe. His face looked as if it had been stung by a million bumble bees. He slurped in the blood from his puffy lips and exhaled. "I'll make it up to you, son. I promise. You'll be filthy rich when it's all said and done. You have my word on that. Now, shoot."

I didn't know what he meant by all of that at the time, but it wouldn't take long for me to find out. I aimed and fired three times, trying my best to hit the target where he'd ordered me to shoot him.

Boom. Boom. Boom. His body jerked forward and then backward three times before he fell on to his side and off the bed, right next to his cell phone that I'd strategically placed there. Finally, I ran out of the house after I wiped the handle of the gun clean and left it in the hallway like he'd told me too.

Chapter 2

"Nigga, you get a hundred and fifty thousand, and fifteen birds. Now if that ain't a muthafuckin come up, I don't know what is!" Paper hollered, popping the cork on his Ace of Spades. The bubbles spilled over his hand. He stopped and sucked them off before dancing with his head tilted backward. "We finna get this money!" he exclaimed.

Aaliyah adjusted herself on my lap, rubbed her cheek against mine before kissing it softly. "That is a lot of money, baby. Soon as you handle this shit with Ken, then I think you should hit the ground running. I got a few hoes I know will help push that product for you, too."

I nodded. " Shit, we got so much work now that you can bring together your own lil' female crew, and we can really expand the way we're supposed to. It's time to get rich. I gotta game plan that won't fail."

She kissed my cheek again. "I'll do whatever you want me to do. All you gotta do is guide me. That's what this shit is all about." She kissed my cheek again as Paper came over and handed her a bottle of champagne. She took off the seal then struggled with the cork, handing the bottle to me.

Thuck! I popped it and allowed the bubbles to fizz over my fingers before handing it to her. "Here you go, ma." I watched as she turned it up. "Paper, before we hit the ground running, you know we gotta handle this business with Ken for her. A deal is a deal," I said standing up and allowing Aaliyah to take my seat. I grabbed my pistol off the table and put it into the small of my back. It was a habit of mine.

Aaliyah had been sold to Ken by her mother when she was only seventeen years old, and he didn't waste any time going in on her and putting her out on the track. Ken was a well-known pimp all throughout the city and surrounding states. He specialized in the selling of young females.

One day, Ken had sent Aaliyah and his bottom bitch, by the name of Meeka, out to work the busy avenue of Lisbon when a few white dudes pulled up and wanted to have unprotected sex with Aaliyah, and she wasn't with it. Then, Meeka tried to force her to do it anyway. Long story short, Aaliyah and Meeka got into a fight in the alley, right off the busy street, and Aaliyah would wind up stabbing Meeka to death. When I rolled up on her, she was just running away from the murder scene. A murder scene that I'd helped her to escape. It and her pimp, Ken.

In the motel where I put her up, we'd made a deal. In exchange for her putting me up on a lick that would help me bully my way into the dope game, I would kill Ken. The man that had already murdered her mother in cold blood.

Paper took a long swallow from his bottle. "Nigga, after all this bread that shorty put us up on, I'm down to do whatever. All you gotta let me know is what's really good. We can body that nigga tonight if need be. What you think, Aaliyah?"

She lowered her head and shrugged before looking up at me. "He run the show. So, whatever he say do is cool by me, just as long as y'all handle that business soon. I can't have this nigga tracking me down and killing me. I'm too young to die." Though it sounded like a joke, I could see that she was dead serious.

I wrapped an arm around her shoulders and shook my head. "Fuck that nigga Ken. Ain't nobody gon' put they hands on you no more. That's my word. You brought us all this shit, that mean that you're a part of this empire that we're about to build from the ground up."

Paper nodded. "If the homey screaming that type of shit, then that mean that I'm riding with you, too. So, give me a hug so we can seal this bond." He reached out and grabbed her hand, pulling her up and into his embrace. "Damn, you smell good." He closed his eyes and sniffed at the top of her head.

She tried to wiggle out of his embrace, but Paper tightened his grip, then trailed his hands down to her ass.

When he cuffed her cheeks, Aaliyah stood on her tippy toes. "Let me go, Paper, that shit ain't cool." She beat at his chest.

I broke them apart and pulled her arm until she was behind me. Then, I mugged the shit out of my right-hand man. "Look, bruh, she been through enough in life with rotten ass, rapist type niggas. We ain't gon' treat her like that. In this empire, she gon' be treated like a queen; you understand me?" I asked, curling my upper lip.

It wasn't that I was down to fight my nigga over Aaliyah because Paper was like my brother. I wasn't about to stand by and watch him treat her like she was trash or something just because of her past profession. In my eyes, we were all in the streets one way or the other, so it wasn't for any of us to judge the other. We had to operate like a family. Respect had to be law, and that was that. No matter if she was a female or not.

Paper looked me deep into the eyes then lowered his own as if he couldn't believe what I was saying. "Bruh, what? You trying to save this bitch or somethin'? When we start doing shit like that?" He set his bottle on the table and stepped within arm's reach of me. I noticed his nostrils flaring.

I could tell that he was heated and maybe even a lil' hurt because I had never stood up for any female when he came at them as reckless as he'd done her.

I shook my head. "Chill that shit out, nigga, and listen to what I'm saying. She is the reason that we got all this shit. Her. The least we can do is give her some respect, loyalty, something, my nigga. I ain't telling you to stop being you. Fuck them other hoes out there, but within this empire, she gon' be our queen. That's all there is to it. Every organization got one, and she's ours."

We looked at each other for a long time before Aaliyah got up the nerve to come from behind me and separate us. She turned to Paper. "Look, Paper, I can tell that you like me, and that's cool. Just come at me with a lil' respect and ain't no tellin' what can transpire. I mean we're all grown here, right?" she asked him, smiling.

Paper looked into her pretty face, and just like I often did, he melted. "Yo, I'm tripping," he said smiling, and pulling her into his arms. "That's my bad. I ain't ever gave a fuck about no bitch, so it's gon' be new to me. But I can try my best to understand where the homey coming from. Y'all just be patient with me. But, please, let me grab this big ass one more time, with your consent, of course." He licked his lips at her.

Aaliyah popped back on her thick legs and looked over her shoulder at me. "What you say, daddy? You know I run under you now, so what's good?"

I looked over to paper and he had this crazy ass pleading look in his eyes that made me want to laugh. I nodded. "It's good, lil' mama. Let the homey feel what our queen is working with."

Paper didn't waste no time. He trailed his big hands from her waist onto the small of her back, then down to her fat ass cheeks that were covered by some tight Prada denims that acted as a second skin. He cuffed her ass cheeks, lifting her a little bit. He leaned into her neck and sucked on the thick vein there, causing her to moan out loud.

"Okay, Paper, that's enough. Ooh, that's enough, boy, stop."

Paper seemed to ignore her, even as she tried to push him away. He ran his hand between her legs from the back, rubbing her monkey, pressing his fingers into the jeans so he could feel it better. "Damn, this muhufucka fat, Aaliyah. You gotta let me hit this shit. Seriously, what's good with it?" He pulled her closer to him and kissed her juicy lips, licking all over them, then sucking them into his mouth.

She shook her head. "N'all. Stop." She moaned, out of breath, kissing him back.

Paper reached between them and unbuttoned her pants, pulling them midway down her thighs. He exposed her thick, brown ass cheeks. They jiggled every time she moved. Then his hands were all over them— pulling them apart. The G-string that separated the globes did very little to shield her nakedness.

Paper sucked on her neck again, moving his hand in between the front of them, trying to go inside of her panties. I really didn't know what to do because on one hand she was saying that she wanted him to stop, but then she kept on kissing him back, and moaning into his mouth. So, I was confused.

"Aaliyah, you good?" I asked.

Paper pressed her up against the wall, dropped down in front of her and yanked her panties down to her ankles. He forced her thighs wide apart and stuck his face in her gap, slurping loudly at her pussy.

"Uhhh! Rich!" She closed her eyes and tilted her head backward. "What is he doing to me?" she moaned.

Paper picked up her left leg and placed it on his shoulder while he ate her pussy like a lesbian. She grabbed a hold of his head and forced it into her box, and it didn't stop Paper from licking up and down her crease and sucking her sex lips into his mouth loudly. He took two fingers and ran them in and out of her box at full speed. I could smell the scent of the soap that she used to keep her kitty fresh. It wafted into the air, along with a hint of her natural pussy's odor. The scent caused my dick to get as hard as a brick.

"Un! Un! Un! Un! Shit, Paper. You gotta stop," she moaned, grabbing the back of his head and riding his face faster and faster. Her thighs jiggled, and her nipples were poking through her Prada blouse so severe that it looked as if they were trying to come through it. She slowly opened her eyes and looked out at me. "I want you too, Rich. Please. I want some of you, too." She humped his face faster and faster.

Paper ran three fingers up her pussy hole. His wrist was a blur. Then, I watched him open her sex lips as wide as they would go, before he sucked her clit into his mouth and nipped at it with his teeth until she was coming all over his face in strong jerks.

"Uh! Uh! Uhhhh!" she screamed and fell forward into him.

Paper was on one knee, going to town on her for another two minutes. Then, he bent her over the chair that we'd been sitting in and took a rubber out of his pocket, tearing it with his teeth, before sliding it over his penis. "I'm finna fuck the shit out of this pussy. This our queen. I'm cool with that." He slapped her on the ass, hard.

"Uh! Just come on, Paper, before I change my mind. Rich, get over here and let me suck that dick, baby," she said, reaching out for me as she bent forward so Paper could get into position.

My dick was throbbing. I ain't gon' even lie. I wanted to fuck her just as bad as Paper did, but it was something in me that felt like it wasn't right. I felt like she was just doing this because she wanted us to accept her, and for me it wasn't about that. I genuinely appreciated her putting us up on that lick with my father, and I understood her past. So, the sexual thing wasn't a priority. I just wanted for me and her to be cool.

But I played it off and laughed. "Nah, ma. Let Paper handle his business, then we'll see what's good after that."

She shook her head and started to get up. "Then fuck that, Rich. If you ain't gon' let me have some part of you, then I ain't doing shit, because I belong to you now." She stood up and pushed Paper away from her, exposing her pussy to my view.

The lips were thick and heavily engorged. They had light traces of pussy juice all over them. There was also a nice amount trailing down her thighs. All of it was a turn on for me, but I was trying to stand my ground.

Paper mugged the shit out of me with anger. His dick laid up against his belly, jerking from need. "Man, come on, bruh. You said she our queen. Shit, you don't think Birdman and Wayne be fucking the shit out of Nicki?" He sucked his teeth loudly.

Aaliyah looked into my eyes and seemed as if she felt a little guilty for what she'd done. "Rich, if I'm bogus just tell me. I thought you'd want me to please y'all. You know, like a queen is supposed to." She lowered her head.

Paper rubbed his hard dick all over her ass cheeks, reached around and grabbed a handful of both of her titties. She moaned out loud and tilted her head back into him. "Let me hit this pussy, Aaliyah. I'm one of the kings, too, so I got a say so in what takes place with you too, ma." He kneeled just a little bit, took his head and placed it on her sex lips.

They spread, ready to accommodate him while he pulled her thick ass cheeks apart.

"Just let me hold your dick then, Rich, while he fucks me. I don't have to suck it or nothing like that. I just need you to know that I'm doing this because of you. I submit to you now, daddy. Okay?" She reached forward and pulled me to her by use of my Ferragamo belt. Once close enough, she unbuckled my pants, reached inside of them and grabbed my hard dick out. "Damn, I knew you was strapped." She stroked me, sniffing the big head. "Uh! Shit."

Paper slid into her pussy and started to fuck her so hard that I thought he was trying to hurt her. He pinned his eyes on her pussy from the back, going to town. *Bam. Bam. Bam. Bam. Bam. Bam. Bam.* He clenched his teeth, moaning deep within his throat. "Arrgh, this shit good, Rich!"

"Un, un, un, un, yes, fuck me! Rich. He fucking me! Un, un. So hard!" She bounced back into him again and again, while her titties shook inside of her blouse with both nipples poking at the fabric. She continued to sniff my pipe, rubbing it all around her pretty face while Paper pounded her out like a mad man.

He fucked her for a full hour, ending by putting her legs over his shoulders and slamming into her while she screamed at the top of her lungs. The whole scene had me feeling some type of way. I wanted to get involved so bad, but the man in me wouldn't allow it. I had too much respect for her and I couldn't help her.

After they got done, Aaliyah went and showered again. When she came out, Paper went inside so he could do his thing. I was loading my money and dope into a duffle bag, so I could transport it to Andrea's house. I couldn't wait to get there so I could get me some pussy for the night. I didn't give a fuck if she was sleep. I was waking her ass up because I had to get right.

Aaliyah walked up to me, putting her hair into a curly ponytail. She was about a foot away when she stopped and looked up at me. "Rich, can I ask you a question?"

I continued to stuff bundle after bundle of cash into my bag before I zipped it up and dropped it to the floor. Then I turned and looked down on her. "What's good, Aaliyah?"

She looked into my eyes and exhaled. "Did you not want to do nothing back there because you think I'm gross or somethin'? Be honest. I guess I could understand that with all things considered." She lowered her head for a moment then slowly looked back up to me.

I smiled, took my hand and gripped the side of her face with it before pulling her into me, kissing her on the forehead. "Queen, it ain't ever nothin' like that. You're my ace and I'm just as attracted to you as Paper is. I just respect you a lil' more, that's all. I know everybody been telling you that sex is the only way for people to love and respect you your whole life, and that ain't the truth. I don't want us to have that kind of a relationship. I need for us to be deeper than that. I want you to be my equal. Like my sister. That's all that is. You could never be gross to me, ma. I got a whole lot of love for you already. That's my word." I held her tight and kissed her lips, running my fingers along her side burns, then smiled at her.

32

She bit into her lower lip before tears started to run down her brown cheeks. "I've never had a man to treat me the way that you do, Rich. You make me feel so weak all the time, and all I want to do is please you and be with you forever. Please don't stop caring about me because I need you. I need your love and affection. It's the only thing that's keeping me going, Rich. Do you hear me?" she asked, looking into my hazel eyes.

I nodded, then kissed her on the forehead. "I got you, boo. Trust and believe that." I wrapped my arms around her, holding her as she continued to cry into my chest. No matter what took place, I was gon' make sure that I was there for her against all odds. Other than me, she ain't really have nobody to lean on, so I started to see her as the filling to the hole that my precious mother had left within me. I had to hold her down.

* * *

When I got to the crib, Andrea was laying in the bed snoring lightly. I came into the room, took off my clothes and climbed under the sheet, taking her gown and forcing it above her waist as I pulled my dick out. I knew that she rarely ever slept with any panties on, and that night was one of the nights that she'd neglected to do so. I placed her right thigh onto my forearm, sucked the side of her neck, lined my dick up, and slid deep into her womb, feeling her heat sear me. Like usual, she was already just a little wet.

"Unn-a, Rich. What you doing, baby?" She tried to look over her shoulder at me.

I attacked the back of her neck and drove into her with force. My eyes were closed tightly, imagining Aaliyah's pussy, remembering how fat and puffy it was, and the way the juices leaked out of it and on to her thick thighs. "Umm, Andrea. Give me this pussy, ma. Let me beat this shit in!" I growled, fucking her hard as we laid on our sides. My dick shot in and out of her at full speed.

She tried to sit up, throwing her big booty back into me. "Fuck me, Rich. Fuck this pussy, lil' daddy. Unn, yes, I love it! Fuck me harder, Rich! Hard as you can, daddy. Unnn-a, fuck!" She hollered as I drove into her with anger. Her thick thighs jiggled just as much as Aaliyah's had. They were both strapped with bodies to die for.

I got on to my knees while she continued to lay on her side, took her right leg and placed it on my shoulders so I could dig deep into her pussy. My pipe stretched her hole wide. Its juices poured out of her and onto my balls, already.

In my mind, in that moment, she was Aaliyah. I didn't know why I couldn't get her out of my mind, but I couldn't. Her body was so righteous to me and I wanted it so bad. Andrea was equally fine, and on a normal night there wouldn't have been any reason for me to have pictured another woman in my head. But the act of Paper and Aaliyah had flipped a switch within me and I had to take it out on Andrea's thick ass.

I leaned down and sucked into her neck while my hips continued to piston into her. A loud smacking noise resonated into the air. Her pussy spat its juices all over my pipe, drenching me. My hips crashed into her ass and I felt my seed getting ready to shoot out of me. I sped up the pace and forced her into a ball, making it impossible for her to move almost.

"Ahhh! Shit, Rich! You're killing me!" She hollered with her legs opened wide and knees pressed to her shoulders.

My dick pounded into her walls, beating at them with hunger. "Grrr, grrr." I growled with my teeth clenched and my back popping, digging at her center. Then, I was cumming harder than I ever had before, as I imagined how Aaliyah's ass looked while Paper pounded into it from behind. In my mind, it had been me.

"Huh, huh, yes! I'm cumming, daddy. I'm cumming. Oooo-a yes, cum in meeee-a!" She screamed.

Chapter 3

Paper turned the heat up on the thermostat because our trap was freezing on the inside. He rubbed his hands together, took a bottle of Patron out of his pocket, twisted the cap off, then drank from it before trying to hand it over to me.

I declined, pushing his hand away. "I'm good. tell yo' lil' niggas to have a seat at the table while I break this work down for them," I said sitting down, and pulling the kilo of cocaine mixed with meth out of my duffle bag.

It was a mixture that Andrea had created that had me and Paper seeing bundles of cash at a time because the fiends couldn't get enough of its high grade. They said it allowed for them to feel as if they were smoking crack for the first time, but instead of the high only lasting for about fifteen minutes, it allowed for them to stay at their highest point for four hours straight, which was unheard of in the crack community. So, at this point, me and Paper had fiends traveling all over the city just so they could come and cop from us. We needed to spread out which was why Paper had snatched up a few young, hungry savages to push our product in their hood.

Macho was a real skinny Puerto Rican and Black kid with curly, black hair that he kept in a ponytail. "Yo, Paper ain't gotta give us no orders that we can follow straight from your mouth, Pa. Since we gon' be working for both of y'all, it's a must that we get to know you, too." He extended his hand. "My name Macho. I'm the leader of my crew. We call ourselves Misfits, and because y'all gon' be putting food on our tables, we pledge allegiance to you and that brother over there. Loyalty is everything, nah'mean?" He shook my hand then gave me a half-hug before doing the same thing to Paper.

Then, Porky stepped forward and did the same thing. "My name Porky, and I'll kill for this nigga right here. We used to take baths in the same sink when we were little. He's the only family I got, and we run our young crew with an iron fist. Y'all help us to eat, and you both will forever have killers in your corner. Trust me on that," Porky said, pulling on his nose. He was a real heavy-set, short, full-blooded Mexican teenager with a shaved head and beady eyes.

Before me and Paper had put their crew down with us, they were known for drive-by shootings and gang banging. Neither Porky nor Macho was older than seventeen, but both had at least five bodies under their belts, meaning that they'd killed at least five people apiece. I was nineteen and only had three.

They sat down at the table, along with the five other members of their crew that was present, while I laid the work out in front of me. I took eighteen ounces and slid it over to Porky, then did the same to Macho. "That's a whole kilo of the Andrea right there. You should be able to make an easy seventy-six thousand from it. All you owe us is forty gees."

Paper nodded. "That A-1 work right there, you ain't gon' be able to hold on to it for long. In fact, y'all should be hollering back at us in like two days. If you come with the full seventy-six, then we'll hit you with two birds. You'll owe us eighty, and seventy-two thousand you'll be able to keep for yourselves, so you can feed your crew. Every time you pop a kilo for us, we'll pay you thirty-six bands. You get that?" Paper asked, pulling out a knot and counting off hundred-dollar bills before sitting them in front of Macho.

Macho frowned and looked him over. "What's this for?" He took the money and began to count it.

"That's ten gees right there. It ain't got nothing to do with the hustling side of things. This money here is for the deadly part of your crew to shut down the other shops that call themselves competing with our operation. I don't give a fuck if you pull kick-doors once a day until all them niggas run to the other side of town. Every time I hear that you shut one of they ass down, it'll be ten gees in it for you, and we'll replace their crew with members from yours until the monopoly is so vast that we're eating and burping at the same time."

Porky sat his chubby hands on the table. "I like the sound of that." He reached under the table and came up with a Mach .11. "Tell me something. What kind of artillery you niggas using for protection around this muhfucka?" He slid the Mach across the table until it wound up in front of me.

I picked it up and popped the clip out, looked it over and slammed the thirty-two-shot magazine back inside of it. "All we got is hand pistols right now. Why what's good?" I set the Mach on the table and looked him over. He pointed at Macho.

Macho smiled. "Because, bro, we got good intel that says those niggas up the street just hit up a sporting goods store and got away with a whole bunch of guns and shit, and we wanna knock 'em off tonight, with your approval of courses, since we are employed by you."

I frowned. "Paper, what's good with homey them up the street? You jam with them or what?" I picked the Mach back up and turned it over in my hand. I liked the way it felt, and I could imagine myself doing some real damage with it. Had I had something like that when Paper's mother came under attack, I was sure that I would have aired out both dudes, and she'd probably still been alive. But then again, I didn't know because when the Reaper came for you, then it was your time to go.

Paper laid both of his hands on the table and leaned in. "All them fools do is sell low quantities of weed. They ain't really no threat. I mean, unless we trying to sew that side of the market up too, which I think we should."

"My uncle got some of the best Hydroponics that the Midwest ever seen, straight from Mexico. I know if I could come to him with a nice amount of money that he'd plug me better than anybody else. He's a businessman, but before anything, he's my blood." Porky took a cigarette from behind his ear and lit it.

I shrugged. "I mean, I ain't trying to turn down no money at all. If you can get us a plug on the weed, Porky, then I'm all for it. I'll put up the cash and we'll go from there. Far as shutting them niggas down and taking their weapons go." I held up the Mach and cocked it with my upper lip curled. "I say y'all do what you gotta do, and for that mission you'll be heavily compensated. Me and the homey fucking with you Misfits the long way. Word is bond."

Macho scrunched his face. "Then we seal this shit right now. We make a pledge of loyalty to one another, only to be broken in death and blood." He scooted away from the table and stood up. Seconds later, the members that he'd brought of his crew did the same thing. "Let's hug it out."

That's just what all of us did.

They left to do their thing, and as soon as they did, me and Paper opened shop and got right to the money. Shirley put the word out that we were back in business after taking a few days off to honor Paper's mother's burial, and it was like less than an hour later our back door was full of hypes. They formed an orderly line at our back door, and me and Paper took turns serving them, one after the next until the wee hours of the morning. By that time, we'd sold out of an entire kilo of the Andrea and had made a little more than seventy-five thousand, due to a few sorts that we'd taken.

Me and paper split the money down the middle, and I got tired and felt like I needed to go back to Andrea's crib to rest for a few hours because over the past week, I might have gotten a little more than twenty hours of sleep total. I was a bit exhausted and I could tell that Paper was too.

As I was placing my money into a Ziploc bag, he came over and plopped down on the couch beside me, exhaling loudly, sipping on a bottle of Hennessy. "You sound as tired as I feel." I yawned, covering my mouth.

He yawned directly after I did and neglected to cover his mouth. "Hell yeah, bruh. I feel like I can sleep for all day. It's been a while." He yawned again. This time he covered his mouth, then took a sip of his liquor.

I stood up and tucked the Ziploc full of money into my pants and pulled my Polo shirt over it. "Yo, I'm 'bout to go and get some rest at Andrea's crib. I'll get up with you tomorrow, bright and early." I pulled him up so I could give him a half-hug.

He hugged me then nodded. "That sound good. I'm tired as hell too. Think I'mma make Shirley suck this dick so I can get some much needed rest as well." He paused and gave me a weird look. "Do it have to be bright and early though? Can we sleep in just a little bit?" He asked with his shoulders slumped forward.

I laughed as my eyes felt like sand bags, then shook my head. "Hell n'all. We on a mission right now. We gotta go hard until we can snatch up some more young niggas to work the trap for us. Right now, we ain't in no position to miss a penny. So, until further notice, this just what it is." I hugged him again and walked toward the front door. "You feel me though?"

He yawned again and covered his mouth. "Yeah, I'm following yo' lead, bruh, even though this shit ain't new to me. Your drive is crazier than mine, but I'mma get there. Oh, and before I forget, I want us to rollout to Memphis to scoop my sister. She moving up here in a few months, but before then, she want us to come down. She still remembers yo' ass too. She asked me was you still crazy." He smiled.

I grunted, adjusting the Ziploc bag of money in my crotch. "When you trying to do this?"

I had not seen Chasity since I was about thirteen years old. She was Paper's older sister. Twenty-one years old, and from what I could remember him telling me, she'd been a stripper down in Memphis for the last three years, though she'd previously left Milwaukee to go down there to attend the University of Memphis. She'd gotten a two-year athletic scholarship to run track. I didn't know how things had panned out for her. She was his half-sister, they shared the same mother, but had different fathers. Her father was Arab, living back in Saudi Arabia. At least that's what Paper had told me.

"I say we hustle hard for the next two weeks, then we take a few days off and go down there and do it big for her. Her birthday is in seventeen days. So, what you say?"

Before I could give him my answer, I heard a series of gunshots somewhere down the block. They stopped for about five seconds, and then there were so many that I flipped the light switch and ducked down. The gunfire continued to erupt. It sounded rapid and as if there was an army movie playing.

Paper ducked down and reached under the couch. I could see him by the light that was shining through the trap's window. He pulled out a forty Glock, cocking it back as more and more gunshots sounded, then there was the screeching of tires.

Shirley came out of the back room with a .38 revolver in her hand. "Who the fuck down there shooting like that?" She asked with her eyes wide and hair all over the place.

Paper stood up and walked into the living room toward her. "I don't know, but they better keep that shit down there," he said, walking toward the window and peeking out of the curtain.

I jumped up and took my Glock out of the small of my back. "Shit, if they did bring it down here, we wouldn't be able to do shit with them. We got these old ass pistols. When we should have some shit like they down there bussing." I felt envious. Me and Paper had to step our game up because it wasn't nothing stopping niggas from getting up with us if they wanted to.

We only had a few hand guns in the trap and they were old, and probably on the verge of jamming or losing their pins. I felt like we were suckers and victims in the making.

Before I could down us even further, I got a text from Macho telling me that it was good, and that the mission was accomplished. It took me a few seconds to understand what he meant, and then all at once it clicked. The niggas down the street had been handled. That made me smile and grow a little bit optimistic.

It didn't take long before there were sirens off in the distance. I hurried and hugged Paper again, then Shirley, and bounced out of the back door, jogging over to my whip that was parked in the garage, directly behind our trap. I was about ten feet away from getting inside when two sets of flashlights were shined on to me.

"Hey, you. Freeze, and don't move," said the person holding one of the flashlights.

My first instinct was take off running. I froze in place and then started to walk backwards, thinking of the best escape route. I was uncomfortable because of the big bag of money stuffed down my pants. I didn't give a fuck what happened, they weren't getting my loot without killing me.

I held up my hands. "Say man, who is that?" I asked getting ready to break into a sprint. I just needed to get a little closer to the gate in our backyard, so I could scale it and break camp. Whoever this was, though, I was guessing they were some form of law enforcement because robbers didn't try and stop you with a flashlight.

I heard a *click-click*. "This is the Milwaukee Police. Do not move one more inch or we will be forced to shoot you. Do I make myself clear?" One of them asked stepping out of the shadows. It was then that I was able to make out that he had his service weapon pinned on me, ready to shoot. He tapped the trigger and a red beam appeared on my chest. I had to look down to discover that.

To his left, another officer with a shotgun appeared, with his gun leveled at me. He didn't say a word. The white man simply frowned and looked as if he couldn't wait until I tried to run or do anything out of the ordinary.

My heart pounded in my chest. I was thinking that I couldn't let them take me in. I'd murdered three people in less than a month, and I didn't know if they knew that or not. I began to panic and thought about risking it all, until my sister's faces popped up in my mind. I had to make the right decisions for them. If the police had anything on me, I felt like me and

Paper had a nice amount of money tucked away. We could spring for a good lawyer, and at the very least get me some sort of bail so I could get out, and then flee on they ass.

The first police with the beam pinned on me started to walk forward more swiftly. "Get down on the ground right now. I'm not gon' say it again, Richard."

Richard? How the fuck did this punk know my name? I thought as I kneeled with my hands in the air.

Chapter 4

I sat in the backseat of the police car with my hands behind my back, cuffed, with the iron so tight on my wrist that I felt like my hands were going numb. Sweat rolled down the side of my face even though it was cold outside. The car drove on with the officers refusing to say anything to me.

"Say, man, what are y'all arresting me for?" I hollered. They'd still not searched me, and I was worried about them finding my money. I knew that the Milwaukee police was dirty as they came.

The officer that had the shotgun pinned on me turned around in his passenger's seat and frowned. He grunted, then turned back around in disgust.

"Yo, y'all ain't even read me my rights. According to the constitution, y'all gotta tell me what I'm being arrested for, and read me my Mirandas." I know that I'd seen that somewhere before, and I knew that to be the truth, but once again, they ignored me, and the car kept on rolling through the night.

They drove all around the city and didn't stop the car until we wound up in the back of a place that bought aluminum and all recycled-like content from the residents of that area. It was located next to some railroad tracks and an abandoned lot. The area was dark and deserted. As soon as the cruiser pulled in, my antennas went all the way up and I felt like panicking.

The driver threw the car in park, got out, came to the back door and threw it open before pulling me by the arm and onto the ground where I'd fallen. "Get up!" he hollered.

I struggled to get to my feet. "Man, what's this all about?" He took me by the back of the head and slammed my face o to the hood of his car, placing his mouth close to my ear. "It's about you selling your drugs in our area and not cutting Uncle Sam into the mix, boy. Don't you know that everybody gotta answer to somebody?" He pushed my face into the hot metal of his hood.

"Ahhh-ah!" I hollered feeling like my face was being melted.

The passenger got out of the car and slammed his door. Taking his shotgun, he lay it on the hood next to my forehead. "My name's Shaw, and I don't like you, Richard. What kind of man moves into a new territory and thinks he's going to take over without greasing a few palms?" He laughed, leaned in and hollered in my ear. "It's the way of the world. If Donald Trump had to grease palms to get into the White House, then you should know that your black ass has too also." He grabbed the back of my neck and squeezed it.

The other officer kicked my legs apart and began to search me, while the other held me down. "You got anything on your person that's going to stick me, boy? Huh?"

I closed my eyes as the pain on the side of my face became so intense that I felt like crying. "N'all, I don't."

He proceeded to pat me down, rubbing up and down my legs, and around my waist, discovering my Glock. "Well, well, well, look at what we have here, Shaw. Looks to me like we've found our shooter." He held the gun outward for Shaw to take from him.

Shaw grabbed the gun and took out the clip, cocking it so that the bullet in the chamber popped out. "It was loaded too, Bradley. I'm guessing this here fella was about to kill one of his own. Ain't that the story?" He laughed.

"Look, man, I ain't got time for these games. If all y'all looking for is money, then we can make some sort of deal. We're all businessmen here." I was ready to end this fucking abuse. I didn't like how them white dudes had me hemmed up. I felt vulnerable and like in any minute they could have killed me.

My fingerprints were all over that gun, and on top of that it had at least two bodies on it. They could have blasted me back there and my body wouldn't have been found until the next morning. In Milwaukee, nobody real gave a fuck about the Black male's life, other than our people, so my murder wouldn't have even been investigated thoroughly. At least that's how I felt.

Bradley turned me around, so I could face him. I looked into his red face and frowned. He grunted, then laughed. "We're just joshing you, Rich. Here, let me take these cuffs off you so we can talk man to man." He turned me around and took the cuffs off my wrist before putting them back onto his belt.

I rubbed my wrists, mugging the shit out of both of them. I still felt like they were up to something. "So, what's it gon' take to get y'all off my ass? I don't do the snitching shit, so never expect that from me. Outside of that, I'm open for suggestion." I inhaled deeply. I'd never been that close to a cop before. I didn't like the smell of them or what they represented. They made me feel sick on the stomach. Shaw took his shotgun and held it up against his shoulder, reaching into the police cruiser and shutting off the head lights that had been on. I could still hear the roaring of the car's engine, and the occasional orders from the dispatcher on their radios.

Bradley stepped in front of me and extended his hand. "I feel like we got off on the wrong foot. My name is Bradley, and I patrol the 53206 area that you and Demetrius work out of. I hear that you're going to be the next big thing coming out of my district, and me and my partner want in." He looked over at Shaw.

Shaw came around and extended his hand as well, and I shook it just like I did Bradley's. I remembered it feeling hot and clammy. I hated it. "Seems that you two have a nice operation getting ready to take off. Couple of the users say your dope is the best in town that you call it, Andrea. Why is that?" He asked smiling.

I shook my head. "Never mind that. Let's talk prices. What's it gon' take to keep us in business?"

Bradley rubbed his chin. "Five grand apiece, weekly." He nodded. "You make sure that we have that every week on time, and we'll see to it that nothing happens to your drug houses. You'll have immunity for as long as we say so."

Now I was rubbing my chin. Ten gees a week didn't sound like much. If you asked me, they were low balling themselves. I had plans on making more than five hundred thousand dollars each day. Especially after we got our heroin spots up and running. "Y'all got a deal. I'll make sure that I have the ten gees for you every Friday morning. That sound cool?" I looked from one on to the next.

They nodded vigorously. Bradley extended his hand again. "That's cool, man, but unfortunately we need an advance. Is there any way that we can receive our first payment tonight? Pretty sure you got it, with that big bundle stuffed down your underwear." He started to laugh. "Didn't think I'd miss that, did you?"

Shaw laughed. "Hope not."

This ended with me getting into the backseat of their car, reaching into my drawers, pulling out the bag of money, and giving them five bands apiece for protection from arrest. They wound up dropping me back off at my car. By the time we got there, police were everywhere because of the shooting down the block. Shaw and Bradley were nice enough to trail me until I made it out of the area. Once I was free and in the clear, I took off straight for Andrea's crib.

* * *

When I got there, I was met by Kesha sitting in the living room in front of her laptop, with her glasses on that I didn't even knew she wore. As I came through the door, she jumped up and walked over to me, wrapping her arms around my waist. "Hey, Rich. How have you been?" She asked stepping onto her tippy toes and kissing me on the cheek. "I've missed you."

I closed the door and locked it while I kept one hand around her small frame. I regretted that I'd neglected to spend an ample amount of time with my sister. I loved her with all my heart. "I've missed you too, lil' mama. How have you been?"

She shrugged. "Tired. I been studying like crazy and doing all these online quizzes. I need to get a good score on the SAT's, so I can create my own destiny. I have to be something in life Rich. This ghetto isn't for me, so I gotta get myself and our family out of before it's too late. Oh, and Keyonna came home last night. I think she still in the bedroom sleeping. Just to give you a heads up, she don't look too good." She exhaled loudly and shook her head in a state of disappointment. She walked back to the couch and sat down on it, placing her fingers onto the home row keys of her laptop, ready to go back to work on it.

At hearing that my other little sister was home, my stomach seemed to do a few somersaults. She'd called herself running away so she could follow behind a pimp's son, by the name of Kendell. Kendell's father was Ken, and Ken was the man that Aaliyah formerly worked under within his stable. After her and his bottom bitch, Meeka, had gotten into an altercation, Aaliyah wound up stabbing her to death. In retaliation, Ken had murdered Aaliyah's mother and threatened to do the same to her whenever he caught her. To have him killed, Aaliyah had given me and Paper a lick that would break us into the dope game. The lick that wound up being that of my father.

I went over and sat beside Kesha, looking her over. "Kesha, I know you are expecting me to run into the other room, so I can see what's good with Keyonna, but I just need you to know that I love you just as much, and that I am proud of you for what you're doing right now. You are my inspiration, and I promise, whatever school you get into, I'm going to be able to pay for all your expenses. I swear you won't have to worry about one single bill. Do you hear me?" I leaned over and kissed her cheek. I wrapped my arm around her shoulders, resting my forehead against hers.

She pushed her laptop back, faced me and smiled. "I know you love me, Rich. I'd never doubt that. It's just that Keyonna needs more tending to than I do. I get it." She shrugged. "You got a lot of weight on your shoulders, big bro. I'm just trying to do my part so that I don't be an additional burden in your life. I love you so much." She kissed my cheek again. "Now, go in there and see what's good with our sister. I'm so worried about her that I can barely think straight."

I stood up, turned my back to her and pulled out the Ziploc bag full of money. Then, I dug inside of it until I pulled out five one hundred-dollar bills and cuffed the Ziploc bag under one arm as I handed the money over to Kesha. "Here, sis. I don't know how much pocket change you got on you, but I want you to have this, just in case you come across anything you might want. You deserve it."

She pushed my hand away politely. "N'all, I'm good, Rich. I still got about eleven thousand in my Chase account from the money that you gave me a few weeks back. I don't need you to keep flooding me with dough. It'll make me lazy. I'll start to feel entitled, and the grind that is within me will dwindle. Plus, I know you had to work your ass off for that. I hate knowing that you're in the streets like that, Rich. You have so much potential. Whatever happened to that book that you started writing a few months back? You know, the one about our lives?" She asked, looking into my eyes.

I shrugged. "I'm still working on it every now and then. It's just that I been so busy lately. I ain't really had time to sit down and get back into it, but I will." I felt like I needed for that to be the truth. Writing had always been an escape for me, especially after my mother passed away. I was accustomed to writing at least a chapter a day. I wanted to finish my book and give my life story to the world just as I lived it.

Kesha placed her laptop onto her lap and started typing. "Well, I've been communicating with this sister down in Texas that is the COO of an urban publishing company by the name of Locked Down Publications, and I've sent her the first four chapters of your book, and she loves it. She's already asking me for the finished manuscript, and willing to pass it over to her CEO to see if they can draw up a contract to put this out. Isn't that inspiring?"

I shook my head. "But I only got ten chapters. It's a lot of work that has to be done, and a lot more story that has to be told before I can even consider sending it down to her." I said, imagining the possibilities. I couldn't believe that somebody was interested in my works. It made me feel somewhat important, like maybe I wasn't destined to die in the trap. Like there was actually life outside of it.

Kesha smiled. "Well, big bro, you need to keep on working on it, so I can help you to reach beyond the slums. You're more than what you think you are. And you can soar higher than you feel your wings will support you. I'm here for you, just like you are for me. Together, we will overcome this ghetto." She sat her laptop back and hugged me again tightly. "You're my inspiration, never forget that."

I finished hugging her, took the five one hundred-dollar bills and sat them under her laptop. "And you're mine. Take this money, and anytime I give you some money you take it and put it up for a later date. You never know what life may bring." I started to walk away from her when I stopped and looked into her hazel eyes. Eyes that we had gotten from our father. "Kesha, I promise I'm gon' finish that book."

She smiled then nodded. "I know, Rich. I know you will." Then, she went back to working on her laptop.

I took my Ziploc bag full of money and placed it on top of the dresser in Andrea's room before walking down the hall. When I got outside of Keyonna's room, I took a deep breath and knocked on the door, then without waiting for a response I turned the knob and pushed it in. What I saw made my heart feel as if it jumped into my throat, and then I felt faint.

There was Keyonna, my little sister, in just her night gown with her head bent over her nightstand, a rolled-up dollar in one hand, tooting up a thick line of dope. She snorted it hard, then sat back and coughed, pulling on her nose, looking over to me like a deer caught in my headlights. "Rich, I can explain."

She started, taking a handkerchief and placing it over the pile of dope.

I stormed over to her bedside and yanked her out of the bed, slamming her back against the wall, breathing heavily into her face with so much anger it felt like I could take off my belt and beat her ass senseless. "What the fuck you think you in here doing, Keyonna?" I growled.

She scrunched her little nose that was the color of red. "Man, Rich, let me go. I don't feel like going through this right now. I just want to chill and feel the groove." She lowered her eyes and licked her lips. She wiped the corners of her mouth.

I frowned. "You wanna what?" I didn't know what the fuck she was talking about. I'd never heard that lingo before, so I didn't know if the groove was a new kind of drug or if she was meaning she just wanted to enjoy her high. Either way, I was pissed the fuck off.

She put her hands up to try and break free of my grasp. "Let me go, Rich! You're not my fucking father!" she screamed. She smacked me so hard that I let her go for a minute. Then, she was attacking me with both fists— hitting me in the face, the chest, the neck, and even kicking at me. "Arrrgh, I hate you. I hate you so much!" More swinging and kicking.

I blocked a few of her punches, grabbed her wrist and slung her down to the bed where I took a seat. Once there, I pulled her over my lap, raised her gown and got to whooping her ass with my hand so hard that it hurt me. *Whap! Whap! Whap! Whap!*

"Arrgh! Arrgh! Argh! Stop! Stop! You're hurting me!" She screamed, wiggling like crazy on my lap, trying to break free. But I wasn't going.

Andrea ran into the room in her negligee, saw what I was doing, stopped and covered her mouth. "Oh my God, Rich, what are you doing to her?" She asked walking closer to the bed.

Keyonna continued to kick her legs wildly. "Get him off me, Andrea! Please! He's hurting me!" She cried.

Whap! Whap! Whap! Whap! More blows rained down on her bare ass cheeks. "She in here doing dope, Andrea! Get the fuck out the room and let me handle my sister!" I hollered, ready to snap. "Now!" I felt my temper getting the best of me.

"No, Rich! That's not how you're going to get her to listen or leave that stuff alone. You're only making it worst. Trust me on this!" She walked over and grabbed my right arm, pulling on it, throwing me off balance.

Keyonna bit into my side and shook her head as if she were a Pit Bull. I could feel her teeth come together in my skin.

I threw her off me. "Fuck, Keyonna! What's the matter with you?" I asked standing up and discovering that I was bleeding.

She bounced off the bed and ran into the corner of her room before sliding down the wall and sitting in a ball.

Kesha came into the room looking bewildered. "What's going on in here?" She looked from a crying Keyonna, then over to me.

"He killed our mother, Kesha. Rich did it. He killed her and now she's gone for the rest of our lives. We're alone and I hate his guts so much because of it." She cried with snot pouring out of her nose. She sniffed it back up and swallowed.

I felt like a knife had been stabbed directly through my heart. I put my hand over my chest and plopped down on the bed, lowering my head. "All this time, Keyonna? You been harboring these feelings about that night all this time?" I asked, confused.

Kesha stepped in front of me. "Wait a minute, Rich, what is she talking about? That doesn't make sense."

Keyonna sniveled and wiped away her tears. "It makes perfect sense. Tell her, Rich."

I felt my eyes get watery and I couldn't even help it. It was all because of how hurt I felt Keyonna was, and the fact that I'd never known it. "Kesha, our mother overdosed off of the dope that I gave her." I said, feeling defeated.

Kesha squinted and shook her head. "But, Rich, that doesn't mean that you killed her. It just means that her body was tired of the abuse and it gave out. I don't think it's anybody's fault. Our mother had a problem, and if she wouldn't have gotten those last hits from you, she would have gotten them from someplace else. You gotta know that." She looked over at Keyonna, walked over and kneeled beside her. "He would never hurt our mother. You saw the same things that I did in that house. Rich was always there for us. Even when she wasn't. So, stop it

Keyonna, just stop it." She grabbed Keyonna's shoulders and shook her.

After a time, Keyonna knocked her hands away and jumped up. "Nobody understands my pain other than Kendell. I'm so sick of all of you." She picked up her Prada pants off the ground and stepped into them. "I'm out of here, and neither of you worry about where I'm going. Rich, if you ever put your hands on me again, I will have you arrested. I'm not kidding either. From this day forth, I don't have a family."

She continued to get dressed while myself, Kesha and Andrea looked her over in silence. I wanted to snatch her ass up so badly and force her to stay home and to listen to me, but I knew that it was a lost cause. She was a grown, eighteen-year-old woman and free to make her own decisions. Looking back on this day I wish I would have done more, but I'm still pretty sure that if I had that things would have still turned out the same way.

I watched her pack her bags, and just as she got ready to leave her room, I grabbed her arm and pulled her into my embrace. She struggled against me for a second but then bowed out when she saw that I wasn't letting her go. "I don't know what you're on, Keyonna, but I just want you to know that I love you, that I will always be here for you and only a call away. I'mma make sure to pass something to your Chase account every week. Maybe after you bump your head a little you'll come home and then we can be a family again."

She pushed her way out of my embrace and sucked her teeth. "Yeah, I guess we'll see." She dragged her bags out of the room and out of the house.

***

It took me some time to get over her departure. For the next eleven days I hustled fourteen hours at a time out in the traps beside Paper and the Misfits. I would literally go as hard as I could until my body felt so exhausted that I would be forced to close my eyelids. I'd sleep for a maximum of three hours and be right back in the traps slanging the Andrea. Paper tried multiple times to find out what was eating at me, but I was so sick over Keyonna that I refused to talk about it. My little sister had me screwed up mentally.

Chapter 5

I copped a 2019 Audi truck two days before we were scheduled to go down to Memphis, so we could meet up with Paper's sister, Chasity. It came black on black, but I had it repainted and customed designed the same day that I had Andrea do the paperwork for me. I had it painted candy black with the red Gucci logo going all through it. My seats were red leather with the Gucci logo in the stitching. I put two nine-inch television in each of my headrests and had two thirteen-inch screens that flipped down in the back, so my passengers could watch a movie or play the video games when they rolled with me. In addition to that, I slapped thirty-two-inch gold Spree-wheels on the Firestone tires and put the red ground effects lights on the bottom of the truck, so it really popped at night. I had about ten people doing the work on my truck, and they were sure to get it done the morning of our trip.

Paper copped a 2019 Range Rover and got nearly the same paint job as I had, but his was blue and black with the blue ground effects on the bottom of it, and the Louis Vuitton logo going all through his paint and leather stitching. He sat his truck on some thirty-inch Fans, all gold.

We made sure that we stopped down at the Grand Avenue mall where we hit up Sak's Fifth Avenue. He got everything Louis and I got everything Gucci before we stopped over at the barbershop and got haircuts, so our waves could be popping.

I got me a few pieces of jewelry as well— a nice Rolex, a bracelet and a fat gold rope to offset my ensemble. I really wasn't a jewelry wearing type of dude, but after I saw how hard Paper was going with his jewels, I had to make sure that I was up to par. I knew them country girls were about to be all over us, and I wanted to shine just as bright as my right-hand man. I felt like I deserved it, especially since it had been a long time since I had actually splurged a lil' bit.

The night before we were scheduled to leave, I went over and checked on Aaliyah. I'd moved her from staying inside of the Super Eight motel, into the Hilton, where I'd paid up her bill for an entire month.

She opened the door with her lips pursed. "So, y'all about to leave me in this whack ass city, huh? Ain't that a bitch." She crossed her arms in front of her chest and gave me an angry look. Then, she slammed the door behind me after I stepped all the way into the room.

I held my arms open, smiling at her. She looked me up and down, exhaled, then walked into my arms, hugging me. "I was finna say. I ain't seen yo' lil' fine ass in two days, and this the first thing you say to me?" I kissed her cheek and took a step back, looking into her face.

She was dressed in some real small booty shorts that were all up in her crease. When she turned around to walk to the bed, I saw that both of her ass cheeks were hanging out of the shorts. They jiggled as she walked, and I couldn't do nothing but shake my head.

Paper had bragged that Aaliyah had some nice, tight and wet pussy too. He talked about it for so long one night that I almost rolled over to where she was and got me some, but then I had to remember that she wasn't a piece of meat. She was the Queen of my empire and a friend close to my heart. That ain't mean that I wasn't attracted to her though. I had a hard time every time I was in the same room with her. Especially when we were alone.

"Rich, I don't think you should be leaving the city without taking care of Ken first. When are you going to hold up your end of the deal?" She sat on the bed and crossed her thick thighs.

I walked over and sat down beside her. "You know I ain't gon' leave you hanging. I'mma handle that nigga, I'm just waiting for the right time." I pulled her head onto my shoulder. Once there I wrapped my arm around her slim waist, then moved closer to her. I loved how she smelled. It was Chanel mixed with her natural scent. It was intoxicating.

She sucked her teeth. "It already feels like you are. I mean, y'all going to Memphis without me. What am I supposed to do while you're gone?" She looked up at me then laid her head back on my shoulder, sighing loudly.

I made her stand up then pulled her once again so that she was straddling me. I held on her small waist, looking into her pretty brown eyes that were set inside of her slanted eyelids. I kissed her juicy lips. "You sounding like you wanna go with us or something. If so, all you gotta do is ask." I leaned my forehead closer to hers and smiled. "So? Do you?"

Our eyes searched each other's. She leaned forward and kissed my lips again, closing her eyes. Moaning into my mouth, her tongue searched for my own and found it just as needy.

"Umm, could I, Rich? Would you really take me with y'all?" She placed her weight on me so that I fell back, then adjusted herself, moving her thick thighs on each side of my waist so that she sat backward on my lap. Her big booty spread and covered my entire lap, giving off its heat. She rubbed my chest and attacked my lips before sucking on my neck and grinding into me.

My dick was so hard that it hurt. It jumped in my Gucci boxers. I reached around and took a hold of her thick ass cheeks, massaging them in my hands while I returned her kisses. "You my Queen, Aaliyah. Of course, you can ride out with the family."

I sucked her lips into my mouth and flipped us over so that she was on the bottom, with her legs wide open. I reached between us and rubbed her pussy through the stretchy material of her boy shorts. Her cat felt meaty and was as hot as a loaf of bread fresh out of the oven.

"Umm, Rich. That feel so good. You make me so happy. Please tell me that we finna fuck right now," she said with a voice filled with lust. She humped upward into my hand, opening her thighs as wide as they would go. "Please, Rich."

I sucked all over her neck and trailed my face downward until the tip of my nose was in between her sex lips, separating them. I had the material of the booty shorts pulled tight, sniffing her pussy through it. She smelled like a woman in heat. All pussy, and it drove me crazy. I sucked one of the lips through the shorts and pulled on it, teasing her.

She raised her hips from the bed and moaned. "Rich, I need you. Please touch me. I need you so, so bad." She squeezed her titties that were encased in a tight pink t-shirt. She rubbed around her nipples in a circular motion before pulling on them and humping into the air.

I yanked her shorts to the side and made her yelp, exposing her bald brown pussy that was darker than the rest of her skin. The sight of it sent chills through my body. I set my nose on her hole and inhaled deeply before opening the lips and licking up and down her crease.

She squeezed her eyelids together and humped into my face. "Rich! Rich! Uhh-a, Rich!" She screamed and came, shaking like crazy. She squeezed her breasts together and ran her tongue all over her lips.

I peeled her pussy lips back further, causing her clit to poke out further. I trapped it and sucked on it so hard that she started to shudder all over again. Her clit seemed to squirt out its juices. It tasted salty and sweet at the same time. I loved it. I sucked harder, slid my hands under her ass and dug my nails into her skin until I made her cum for the third time. Then, I sat up and wiped my mouth with my dick pitching a tent, throbbing in my Gucci jeans.

Aaliyah rubbed her thighs together then put her hand between her legs and pinched her clit, rubbing it in a circle. "Let me return the favor, Rich. Please. Just let me taste you," she begged, sliding a finger deep into her pussy. Her shorts were pulled to one side, so I could see her finger clearly going in and out of her wet box. Her juices oozed down her thighs and wet the sheets underneath her.

I wanted to get back down and taste her some more. I had her essence on my tongue and it was making me insane. I don't know what it was about her. I squeezed my dick through my jeans. "I'm trying my best to not go there with you, Aaliyah, but you making this shit so hard." I groaned.

She spread her sex lips apart with her fingers, showing me her pink. "You ain't gotta fuck me, Rich. I just wanna taste you like you did me. Is that too much to ask?" She trailed her hand up and pulled her t-shirt up, exposing both of her pretty titties with the big brown nipples.

I exhaled loudly, walked over to her and pulled my piece out, stroking it while I looked at her fat pussy that had light hair starting to come back on it as if she hadn't shaved it in a couple of days. I extended my hand and rubbed all over it. "Damn, it's something about you, Aaliyah." I slid two fingers deep into her cat.

She pulled me closer using my dick and slid him into her mouth, sucking me hard with her jaws hollowed out, moaning all around my pipe before popping him out. "I love when you touch me, Rich. I swear I love it so much." She sucked me back into her mouth and got to spearing her head into my lap at full speed, slurping all over it. Saliva dripped from my pole and landed on her chin.

I pinched her nipple, pulling it and watching it spring up. Her breasts were nice and round with light freckles all over them. I wanted to suck them so bad, but she had me going through a thing. Her head game was the best I had ever had at that time. I was humping into her mouth as she pursed her lips together, making it nice and tight.

The heat from inside was almost too much to bare. "Unh! Unh! Aaliyah." I groaned, watching her titties shake. I felt my seed rising within me.

She took her hands away and speared her head faster and faster, taking me to the back of her throat before pulling it out and sucking me back in. When she opened her thighs wide, so my fingers could sink all the way into her hot, pink hole, I couldn't take it anymore. I tensed up and let my seed fly.

"Unh! Unh! Unh!" I groaned with my stomach jerking as I came hard into her sucking mouth, feeling my knees buckling under me.

She pumped my pipe until all my seed was out of me. Then, she tightened her fist around the base and stroked it to the top, creating a drip of my cream before licking it off and looking up at me with a smile on her face. "I love yo' taste, Rich. I think we gon' wind up driving each other crazy. Just watch."

* * *

An hour later, I watched her take $7,000 worth of clothes and shoes up to the cashier before I came alongside her and pulled out a knot of hundreds and paid the bill for her. We'd decided that she was going to come along to Memphis with us, and I wanted to make sure that she was just as fresh. So, I let her go crazy in the store. I liked seeing her smile. I don't think she'd ever been spoiled before and I felt good doing it.

After shopping for clothes, I took her over to Jared's and put a few diamonds in her ears, and Diamond tennis bracelets on both wrists before slipping ten gees in her purse. "Here. I want you to hold on to this chump change. Me and Paper gon' be down here acting a fool, and I want you to have the ability to do the same. You're the Queen; you understand me?" I asked as the jeweler placed the pink lemonade diamonds into her earlobes.

She smiled. "I love you, Rich. Let me just make that known right now. I love you, and I ain't never met a man like you before."

* * *

We got on the road at eight o'clock that night. Paper wanted Aaliyah to roll with him, but she insisted on jumping in the Audi truck with me, and I was cool with that. Paper wound up solo for the trip, and I think he was a little irritated by that because he was feeling Aaliyah a little more than she was feeling him. At least that's the vibe that I got.

After stopping at John Red Hots and getting us a couple Gyros, chili cheese fries, two Italian beefs dipped and Sprite sodas, we hit up the interstate with Aaliyah singing in the background, bellowing out of my speakers.

I looked over at Aaliyah and smiled as she sang along with the song. She was dressed in a tight purple and black Gucci dress, with the purple and black, red bottomed Louis Vuitton ankle boots, with the zipper on the sides of them. Most of her brown thighs were exposed and I just had to admire how bad this female was. In my opinion, she was killing the game. I hadn't seen many that were physically on her level, and I was trying my best to not allow that to affect me for the negative because I was seriously attracted to her more than I realized.

She looked over to me and smiled, nodding to the Four Page Letter song that beat out of the speakers, then she turned the music down, looking me over closely. "Why you keep looking at me like that, Rich?" She squinted, and that made her look even more sexy to me.

I laughed and shook my head. "You want me to be honest with you?" I looked out to the highway and then back to her.

She nodded. "Of course. That's all I ask is your honesty in every situation." She made a move in my leather seats that caused her short skirt to rise on her thighs.

I peeped how oily and smooth they were, then thought back on how I watched her apply baby oil to them. They were still popping. I loved a clean and well put together woman. It was my weakness.

"I was over here peeping how your skirt keeps riding up your thighs, and how much that shit killing me. I been hard ever since we hit the highway." I looked into her eyes then back out onto the road. "I was also saying to myself that I don't think I've ever seen a female as cold as you." I looked over at her and into her brown eyes.

She blushed and turned her head so that she was looking out of the passenger's window. "Rich, you always make me feel more than I really am. Do you know that?" She exhaled. "I know I can't be as beautiful as you make me out to be, but whenever I'm with you, I always feel like the baddest chick on the planet. I appreciate your love for me so much. I hope you know that."

I nodded. "Aaliyah, you are the baddest chick on the planet, and until you get that through your head I'm gon' keep on reminding you of that." I reached over and squeezed her thick thigh. "I love you too, by the way. I know you said it the other night and I ain't really respond to it, but I really do. I just want us to be the best of friends, and whatever else we wanna be when we wanna be it. No strings, just free, but bound by one another. Does that make sense to you?" I asked, looking over at her pretty face.

She lowered her head and nodded. "I get what you're saying. It's like we're free to roam throughout this world, but at the end of the day when the world has gotten us down, we should always know that the other is there with arms wide open, ready and willing to hold us down. Right?" She asked, picking her head up, blushing and looking out onto the road.

I nodded. "Yeah, that's exactly what I mean. No matter what goes on in life, I'll be there for you and I'll always have your back, against all odds."

She smiled then exhaled. "You ever think we'll get tired of the world and just want to be with each other? You know, loving the way other people do?" She asked this question refusing to make eye contact with me.

I shrugged. "I think we're just young right now, and we don't have all of the answers. Only thing I know for sure is that I care about you a great deal, and I'm not playing when it comes to you. I'll body a nigga with no remorse over you, Aaliyah. You been through a lot, and it's my job to try and heal you as best I can. That's what true friends are for."

She lowered her head and sucked on her bottom lip. "Ain't nobody ever cared about me, Rich. I never felt that I could mean something to a person, but you say these things to me all the time. You make me feel so special, whereas before you came into the picture, all I saw myself as being was a worthless hoe with no sense of purpose or reason for being. But now, it's like I want to make you proud. I want to do everything that I can so that you love me, because I need you, Rich." She blinked tears. "I need you so, so bad, and I'm so afraid that one day you'll wake up and see me as the world sees me. Whenever that happens, it'll be the day that I no longer want to breathe." She covered her face with her hands and started to cry harder. After a minute of this, she popped her head up and took a deep breath with tears running down her cheeks. "I shouldn't have said that, Rich, but it's the truth."

I grabbed ahold of her hand and interlocked my fingers within hers. "You ain't gotta worry about my love for you changing, Aaliyah. I see you, just like you see me." I shook my head. "I know that we need each other."

She wiped her tears away and laughed. "Yeah, I guess you're right."

Chapter 6

We pulled up in front of Paper's sister's crib at eleven in the morning the next day. The sun was already beaming, and it was so hot that as soon as I rolled down my window, so Paper could hear what I was saying, the heat caused my forehead to perspire.

Paper took a white towel and wiped his face. "Damn, it's hot out here, bruh. Let me run over and knock on the door and get her ass up so we can go straight in. I ain't trying to be out here in this sun." He dabbed at his face again. Then, he looked past me and over to Aaliyah. "What's good, Queen? You missed me?" He smiled and licked his lips.

She yawned and reached her hands over her head as far as they would go, arching her back. "Uuuhh-a!" She covered her mouth. "Yeah, I missed you, Paper. How are you feeling this morning?"

He sucked his teeth and looked her up and down. "I'mma be feelin' a lot better once you and I spend some time down here together."

She nodded and smiled.

I looked over at Aaliyah and we made eye contact.

She lowered her head. "Yeah, I guess we'll see."

Paper frowned. "See? Shit, after all the money we done spent on yo' ass, you talking about we'll see. N'all, seeing ain't got shit to do with it." He shook his head.

I mugged him. "Bruh, chill with that shit. We ain't spend nothing on her that didn't belong to her. She deserved everything she got, and its more where that came from." I looked over into Aaliyah's eyes. "You hear me, Queen?"

She nodded. "Loud and clear."

Paper waved us off. "It's a conspiracy." He laughed. "Anyway, I'm trying to get up with you later, so make some time for me, and don't spend all of your time up Rich's ass." He blew air through his teeth and jogged up Chasity's porch before ringing the doorbell and dusting his clothes off. He pulled his sleeve backward to expose his Rolex and bracelet.

I reached over and squeezed Aaliyah's hand. "You okay?"

She nodded. "I just need to hear you tell me you love me again, and I'll be good. I already know you finna be fucking with plenty of these country girls, and I'mma try my best to stay in the friend zone and not get jealous. You got me feeling some type of way, though. Ah, and what do I do about Paper wanting to be with me on that level? Is that cool with you, or is that weird if we get down again?"

Just then, I saw the door of Chasity's two-story house open, and the porch was flooded with women wearing skimpy shorts and tops. They gathered around Paper and got to showing him all kinds of affection before he pointed to my truck.

"First of all, I love you. Secondly, I do plan on having a good time down here, but I ain't that type of nigga to be fucking a bunch of random broads. I care about my health more than that. Third, if you feeling like you wanna give the homey some more of that pussy, it's cool with me. We're all a family, and it is what it is. You still my baby, and I got you. You hear me?"

She nodded. "I love you too, Rich. I'll be glad when You're wanting me in the way that he is. After you enter my body, I ain't ever letting another man touch me. That's on my mother's grave." She leaned over, and we hugged before I kissed her on the lips.

Looking over her shoulder, I saw Chasity coming down the stairs with some very short shorts on, exposing too much of her golden thighs. When she got down on the concrete, she ran around my truck to the driver's side, trying to pry open the door.

"Here we go with this shit." Aaliyah mumbled.

Chasity knocked on the window. "Rich. Rich, you better get yo' ass out here and give me a hug, lil' bro. I ain't playing with you." She took a step back and crossed her arms in front of her, waiting on me to open the door.

I looked over at Aaliyah. "We're good, right?"

She flared her nostrils and looked off. "Yeah, I guess so. Just don't forget about me while we're down here."

"I won't." I opened the door and stepped out into the hot ass sun. I opened my arms and Chasity ran into them.

I couldn't believe how short she was. The last time I'd seen her, she had been taller than me. Now, she was up under my chin.

She hugged me tight. "Oh my God, Rich, look at you. You got all these fucking muscles, smelling all good and stuff. Umm, where has the time gone?" She nestled her face into my chest, and I could hear her inhaling my scents deeply. She took a step back and I was able to look her over closely.

In my opinion, she looked like a darker, way thicker version of Ariana Grande. Her long hair was pulled back into a pony tail and her baby hairs along her forehead were wavy, along with her hint of side burn. She had a mole on the left side of her lip and her eyes were light brown. Though she was mixed with Arab and Black, her Arab features were prominent in her face, but from the neck down, that was all sista. She was strapped. Thick as they came with a flat tummy and an innie belly button that was pierced. She smelled like Vanilla.

I looked down on her and smiled. "Yeah, I ain't that lil' boy that you used to mess with no more. I'm grown as hell now, and I came down here with the homey, so I could see you. I got this for your birthday." I stuck my head back into my truck as Paper helped Aaliyah out of it and went under my seat and came up with the Jared's jewelry box, handing it to her. "Happy Birthday."

She squealed, snatched the box out of my hand and opened it. "Oh my God! You didn't, Rich!" She threw her arms around my neck and took a step back, looking down at the female Rolex watch that I'd spent fifteen gees on. It was iced with pink and light blue diamonds. She moved the box around so that the sun light could make it twinkle with its rays.

"I remember you always said that you couldn't decide whether pink or light blue was your favorite color, so I just thought I'd have the watch sprayed with both. If there is anything else I can get for you, let me know. I wanna make sure you're good while I'm down here."

She looked up at me and lowered her eyes, sucking on her bottom lip. "Damn, we gotta dip off and catch up, playboy. I see you all about your money now, and that lil' kid shit is out the window, so I got some things that I'd like to run by you." She licked her lips before sucking back on the bottom one.

I closed my truck's door and made my way up the stairs with Chasity's arm around my lower waist. We made it into the house and that's when I was flooded with a sea of women of all different races.

Chasity held her hand up right away to stop them. "Hold on now, let me let you hoes know off the back that it ain't going down like that. Now, this fine ass nigga belongs to me for the weekend. He done came all the way down here to celebrate my birthday, which means that it's all about me. Y'all get that?" she asked.

One thick ass female with some red boy short panties on that looked too small, slapped her hand on her hip and rolled her eyes. She looked as if she were mixed with Puerto Rican and Black, like Andrea. "Damn, Chasity, you always on that selfish shit. I'm trying to see what's good with him too. He fine as hell, and what color are your eyes?" she asked, walking up on me and looking into them. She smelled like Burberry perfume.

I laughed. "They hazel. I got 'em from my old man. He's Italian."

She licked her lips and looked me up and down. "And that truck out there? Is it yours?" She looked over my shoulder and out of the window before looking into my eyes with her intimidating stare.

I nodded. "Yeah, it was a lil' treat to me. I worked hard for it. Why?"

She sucked her teeth and ran her long tongue all over her juicy lips. "Oh, no reason. Just wanted to know. That's all. By the way, my name is Heaven. It's a pleasure to meet you, and regardless to what Chasity talking about, we're going to get further acquainted. Trust me on that."

Chasity stepped in and blocked our paths. I ain't even gone lie, I was getting lost looking at this fine ass chick. "Rich, don't listen to what she talking about. She just think she the shit and can get any man that she want." She mugged Heaven and rolled her eyes, then started to introduce me to the other females that were present.

All of them were strapped with big booties, thick thighs and jazzy personalities. I got to digging them country girls right away. Especially the way they talked. That shit was so sexy to me, and they seemed to love my proper speech as well.

After I was introduced to everybody, Chasity took my hand and pulled me up the stairs, leading me to where she wanted me to follow. Before we made it up, I looked down to the bottom of the flight and saw Aaliyah looking up at me, before she lowered her head and sat down on the couch. It made me feel a lil' sad because I didn't want her to feel like I was going to neglect her or something.

When we got upstairs, Chasity lead me to her bedroom and closed the door. "You can sit in that chair right there," she said, pointing to a love seat.

I walked over to it, looking all around the neatly decorated room. It was decked out with

Burberry everything. She had a seventy-two-inch flat screen hanging on the wall that had a blue screen as if she'd just taken out a DVD or something. "You got a nice room. It's neat. I like that."

She turned her back to me and opened her dresser drawer, pulling out a box of Garcia Vegas, setting it on top of the dresser. It was then that I looked down and saw how her shorts were deep into the crack of her ass. She popped back on her legs and smiled, looking over her shoulder at me. "I got this yellow weed from Miami that's fire. You gotta try it." She pulled out a blunt and reached into the box, came up with a lighter, sparking it. She took three deep pulls before passing it to me. "Try that."

I took it as she walked over to her entertainment system and started the music, banging Cardi B's new album. Then, she walked over to me and leaned over into my face.

"You done got fine as hell, Rich. I didn't think you was gone turn out this handsome, playboy. You already know before you go back up north, me and you gotta tear these sheets up." She leaned forward and licked my lips. "You still got that crush on me?"

I took two strong pulls from the blunt and held the smoke before blowing it back out and setting the blunt in the ashtray to my right. The way she was bent over, I could see down her tank top, all the way to her two big brown nipples. Her titties were a nice shade of golden brown.

I reached up and cupped them, squeezing the globes and sucking on her juicy lips while she moaned into my mouth. "Hell yeah, I do." I licked all over her lips before sucking them into my mouth. I raised her shirt just enough for me to see her breasts in their free form.

She straddled my lap, placing a knee on each side of me, sitting her ass on my pipe. I reached around and rubbed all over the exposed cheeks before sucking on her neck. "Mmmm. Yeah. You remember when we were little, Rich, and I'd always catch you peeking into my room when I stayed with my mother?" She humped forward, grinding on my hard pipe.

"Yeah. I'd always wait until you took them tight ass jeans off. You loved walking around in your panties." I cuffed my hand under her ass and slid my fingers into her leg holes, rubbing her bald pussy, trying to find the hole. She was wet already.

She spread her thick thighs wider and arched her back, kissing my lips. "I knew you was peeking, Rich, and I wanted you to see me. It turned me on knowing that you were dying to see my body, even though I was so shy at that age and insecure. You drove me crazy." She leaned all the way forward with her ass in the air. Then, she took her leg and placed her foot on the arm of the couch, grabbed my hand and forced it down the front of her shorts, where she was without panties. "Unnn! Shit!"

I started rubbing right away, with my eyes closed. Thinking back on them days where I'd spend a night at Paper's crib, she'd be walking around with the tightest pair of Capris on. Her ass was always so big, even back then. I was just a lil' kid and shy as hell, so I reduced myself to peeking into her room when I thought she wasn't paying attention. Then, when I got a good glance of her in the bare minimums, I'd go to the bathroom and do the most to myself with her on my mind.

I opened her sex lips with my two fingers and slid my middle digit deep into her center, feeling her hole suck at it. "Damn, you tight, Chasity." I moaned as she licked all over my neck.

"My nigga been locked up for three years now, so I ain't had no dick. He was supposed to be out next month, but the Feds just indicted him on some old shit, which is why I'm moving up there to where y'all at. I'm so horny. I feel like I can scream," she said with a raspy voice.

I stood up, picking her up with me before throwing her on the bed and coming out of my tops, leaving on my gold ropes. "Man, you got me heated. Look how hard my pipe is." I grabbed it, showing her its tent.

She laid on her back, spread her thighs and laughed, biting on her bottom lip. "I'm saying, you been wanting to fuck me ever since we were kids, so what you gon' do about it?" She climbed on all fours and laid her head on the bed, with her ass in the air, waving it from side to side before pulling the shorts forward and making the material go all up in her ass. "Unh!" she moaned, looking back at me.

It was like the weed kicked in at the same time my hunger for her body did. I was already still kind of riled up from the oral sex that me and Aaliyah had, but now I was feening for some pussy, and I had been lusting after Chasity for years.

So, before I could even stop myself, I snapped. I reached and pulled her shorts down roughly, exposing that fat ass. The cheeks jiggled, and her pussy popped out at me, yet she remained on all fours like a good girl.

"Come on, Rich. You know you wanna fuck me. You better hurry up before Paper come looking for us. I ain't had no dick in three years. Look at this." She reached under herself and opened her sex lips wide, enticing me.

I almost broke my neck sticking my face in it. I took my nose and tried to stuff it into her lil' hole; sniffing her up before licking up and down her crease in a frenzy. I was making so many noises that I felt embarrassed.

"Unn, unn, unn, fuck me, Rich! Hurry up. I need it, lil' bro."

Before she could even finish that sentence, I was sliding a condom on my pipe. I got behind her, put my head on her opening, and slammed into her with so much force. I fucked her as hard as I could while she bit on and screamed into the pillow at the top of her lungs. Her fat ass clapped into my lower abs, wetting me. She pounded back into me, matching my every thrust.

Her pussy was as tight as advertised. I could tell that it had been a minute because it felt like I was fucking a closed, wet fist.

She spread her thighs wide as I went crazy in her womb. "Mmm! Mmm! Mmm! Mmm! Oh my God. Oh my God. Oh my God!" She moaned slamming back into me.

I looked down and watched her pussy eat at my dick, sucking it into her body with hunger. I grabbed her hips and pounded her out; imagining scenes from when we were kids and bringing it back to the present. Apart of me couldn't believe that I was fucking Paper's sister. It felt forbidden and a little wrong. Especially knowing that the homey was in the same house we were getting down in.

"Put your thumb in my ass, Rich, and I'm going to cum. Put your thumb in my ass, Rich, please!" She moaned loudly and slammed back into me.

I slipped my dick out of her pussy and slid into her ass in one stroke while she played with her clitoris, moaning and jerking. She fell to the bed on her stomach with me going in and out of her at full speed. Seconds later I was coming hard.

The door to her bedroom opened, and Heaven came in and closed the door behind her. "Damn, y'all ain't waste no time at all, did you?" she asked, watching my pipe go in and out of Chasity.

I pulled it out and stroked it until all my nut was in the condom. Then, I pulled it off and tied it in a knot, showing Heaven what I was working with on purpose. Like I said before, she was fine.

"Get out of my room, Heaven!" Chasity hollered out of breath.

Heaven sucked on her bottom lip and walked closer to the bed, sniffing the air. "You gotta let this city nigga fuck me one time before he go, Chasity. Shit, we can do him together. Just let me see what that's like." She started to rub the front of her red boy shorts, forcing the material to get trapped into her sex lips. She never took her eyes away from my pipe.

Chasity flipped onto her back and rubbed her thighs together. "Not right now. We'll see what's good later. I still gotta talk to him about some things.

So, get! I'm not gon' tell you again," she warned, sitting up with an angry scowl on her face.

Heaven sucked her teeth. "Dang, you know these niggas down here ain't on shit. All they do is drink that Lean and pass the fuck out. It's some good dick around now, and you trying to hold that shit to your chest. Bet bitch." She rolled her eyes and left the room with her boy shorts all up in her ass. It looked real good to me, too.

Chasity shook her head, mugging the door for a little while, even though Heaven had already gone through it. Then she turned to me and held her arms open. "C'mere, Rich."

I held up the condom. "Where you want me to put this?"

She pointed at the bathroom that was connected to her room. "It's a trash can in there. Just drop it in there and come back so I can feel my body up against yours."

I did just that, then climbed into the bed. As soon as I did, she straddled me and placed her hands on my chest. Her hot pussy was on top of my stomach, searing me.

"How does it feel to have finally been able to get some of this?" she asked, looking into my eyes.

I reached down and rubbed all over her big globes once again. "You got some fire. I can see myself dipping in this pool a whole lot." I leaned up and kissed her hard nipples that were poking through her shirt.

"Well, that's good because I'm trying to fuck with you when I get up there. So, I hope you ain't fucking with a bunch of other hoes. I know you got the pussy on the first day down here and shit, but I been knowing you my whole life, so it ain't like that." She kissed my lips. "Well, do you got a bunch of hoes up there? And don't lie either."

I shook my head. "N'all, I'm still talking to Andrea, but we ain't in no relationship or nothing like that. Honestly, this the first piece of pussy that I've gotten outside of her in a long time. So, it's good." I gripped her ass cheeks. "You think you about to come up there on some possessive shit, huh?" I pulled her down until her lips were resting on mine.

She licked them. "I'm saying, I'm trying to come up there and get money with you. I don't mind staying in my lane, but I ain't trying to be whooping a bunch of bitches over you because they thinking it's more than what it is." She bit my top lip and sat up. "But for real though, I wanna run this shit by you, so let's shower and get dressed."

Chapter 7

It was an hour later, and found myself sitting at Chasity's round table, along with Paper and Heaven. There were two bottles of Patron opened and a pile of yellow weed that Chasity had copped from one of Heaven's plugs out of Miami. I was in the middle of rolling me a fat ass Garcia Vega while I listened to her. In the background, Money Bag Yo banged out of the speakers, and Paper sat directly across from me, sipping from his glass of liquor. His eyes were blood shot, and low.

"So, what I'm saying is that my trick just finalized the deal and purchased that building right there on the corner of Sixteenth and North Avenue. You know, right where that grocery store called Galast used to be. Well, me and Heaven want to turn it into a strip club, but we gon' need some financial help in order for it to do what it do and be a success," said Chasity, stopping to take a sip from her glass of Patron.

Heaved licked her lips and looked from Paper to me. "We can tell you players got plenty of money. Y'all rolling down here on thirty-inch rims and shit, when most niggas scared to hit the highway with their shit. I think investing in us is a great move. We got hoes that's ready to leave Memphis. Bitches that'll come up there and have them city slickers on their backs. Ain't nothing but skinny hoes up there. We gon' bring that southern hospitality amongst other things. Get this paper the right way, know what I'm saying, Dirty?" She started to break a blunt down the middle, preparing it so she could fill it with some of the yellow weed that had me lit.

"How much money we talking?" I asked, passing the blunt across the table to Paper. I had to wave it a couple times in front of his face before he saw it.

Chasity inhaled and slowly blew the smoke out. "We need a hundred thousand. But, we'll be willing to pay back a hundred and fifty grand, no later than two years."

Paper shook his head. "I love the fuck out of you, Chasity, but I don't know if it's a hunnit thousand-dollar kind of love." He snickered, taking a strong pull from the blunt. "I ain't playing neither. Me and the homey got our hands tied up in all kinds of shit right now. To trick off a hunnit gees just so you hoes can come up there and do the same shit you doing down here, it don't make sense to me."

Chasity shook her head. "Here we go with this disrespectful shit. I see you ain't changed one bit. You still got that filthy ass mouth." She rolled her eyes. "You supposed to be my brother. I shouldn't have to convince you to invest in me. You should want to just because of our blood."

Paper shook his head. "Hell n'all. I'm about my money, hence the name. I ain't got no cash to be throwing away. If you thinking this business move is going to be so much of a success, then why don't you hoes got that kind of bread right now? You been down here stripping for three years now. What gives?"

Chasity flared her nostrils and looked down at the table. I could tell that she was trying to control her anger. "I ain't about to argue with you, Paper. If the answer is no, then it's good. Life goes on and I'll figure something else out." She scooted away from the table and made her way up the stairs with her head hanging.

Paper shrugged. "I don't give a fuck, bruh. She can have an attitude. I love my sister, but I ain't about to trick off no major chips for a pipe dream. Ain't no return in that. I'm trying to triple my money at all times." He puffed on the Vega and inhaled with his teeth clenched together.

Heaven looked him over in disgust. "Damn, nigga, that's your sister. What type of man are you? You didn't even stop to ask her game plan. Did you know that she has two degrees for business management and administration? That she been going to school for all of this, and that with her heart and her mind I know for a fact that she's going to be a success. But you're her brother. The nigga she been bragging on, and you come down here and ain't on shit." She curled her upper lip and shook her head, taking her glass of Patron and putting it to her lips.

Paper passed me the blunt before standing up, going in his pocket and pulling out a fist of hundreds. Then, he looked into her eyes and laughed. "Run that drag on some trick ass nigga, not a boss. Here, bitch!" He threw the money into her face, took the bottle of Patron and poured it over her head while she held her hands up, stunned.

I scooted away from the table and made my way up the stairs before knocking on Chasity's bedroom door.

"Who is it?" she asked. She sounded as if she'd been crying or something.

"It's Rich, sis. Let me holler at you for a minute," I said, getting ready to turn the knob.

"It's open, Rich. Come on in."

Aaliyah came out of the bathroom down the hall and held up a finger. "When you're done, I need to holler at you. Okay?" She whispered from a far.

"I got you, boo." I said, pushing in Chasity's door and closing it behind me.

She was sitting in the middle of the bed with stacks of money all around her that had rubber bands on them. I saw that on the floor next to the dresser was a small safe, and it was opened. "This two hundred gees right here, Rich. I don't know why my brother think I'm some lame ass bitch or something. But fuck him. I don't need him. I'll handle this shit on my own like a boss." She looked up at me and I could see the streak of dried tears along her cheeks.

I stepped over and kneeled in front of her. "I'll back you. If you really feeling like you can come back to the city, open a strip club and get that bitch popping, then I wanna have my hand in that. But I don't want to give you a loan. I want to be your partner. We do this shit fifty-fifty, what you say?"

She swallowed hard and looked down on me with watery eyes. "If you back me up on this, Rich, I promise you won't be sorry. I know how to get money. I just gotta be my own boss."

I stood up and pulled her into my embrace, wrapping her arms around me before leaning down and placing my lips on her ear. "I got you. You do whatever it takes to put everything in motion. Let me know when you'll need that hunnit racks and it's yours. Fifty-fifty, though. We gotta put all this on paper. Cool with you?" I asked, hugging her tight.

"Yeah, that's good. Thank you. I got this. I won't fail you, Rich. You'll see."

***

Before I left Memphis, we handled all the paperwork, and me and Chasity went in on this strip club as equal partners. But that night, Chasity threw a pajama party and invited some of the baddest bitches and most up top niggas in Memphis, and surrounding areas. By about ten that night, her house was jumping and there were all types of scantily-clad people walking around with big blunts and bottles of champagne in their hands. The music was all Yo Gotti and Cardi B. The women were shaking their asses hard to the beat, while the niggas held their bottles in the air and made it rain with twenties and fifty-dollar bills.

I placed my back on the wall while Chasity bent all the way over and twerked on my pipe. She was dressed in a real short red, Burberry night gown that came just below her waist. It exposed her red Burberry, lace panties every time she moved the slightest. I pulled the gown up a lil' bit so I could watch her ass cheeks rubbing up against my Gucci, silk boxers.

She looked over her shoulder at me and licked her lips as the music banged in my ears so loud that they were ringing. "You like that daddy?" She hollered, grinding on me real good.

I nodded and bit into my bottom lip. It felt like she was jacking me off with her ass cheeks. I was ready to cum; it was crazy.

There were couples all around getting freaky, dancing with her stripper friends, and they were doing the most. I looked across the living room and my eyes bugged out of my head when I saw Paper and Heaven tonguing each other down. He had his hand in her see through, white Fendi panties, fingering her at full speed, while they kissed all over each other. I placed my hands on Chasity's waist and continued to let her twerk on me in slow motion. Her thick thighs shook as she did her thing, making my dick jump even more.

One of her dark-skinned friends with deep dimples strolled over and kissed me on the cheek before sliding her tongue in my ear. "I got Mollies. You want one?" she asked, then ran her hand all over my chest, biting me on the shoulder as if she were in heat.

Before I could shake my head and tell her I was good, Chasity stood up and turned around so that she was facing her head-on. "Eve, you better gone. I already told y'all that this right here is me." She placed her hand on my chest, then kissed me on the cheek while eyeing her friend.

Eve popped her head backward as if she were offended. "Damn, you was serious about that?" she asked, frowning and putting her right hand on her waist.

Behind her, I could see Paper and Heaven still going at it. Now she had her hand down his boxers while he fingered her, causing her to tilt her head back and leave her mouth open in bliss. They were not the only ones going at it like that. There were actually a few couples that were having sex right there in the middle of the room like it was the most natural thing in the world. This party was lit.

Chasity nodded. "Hell yeah, I'm serious, so gone. He good. If he want some pills, I got my own collection. You forget we got the same plug?" She rolled her eyes and waved Eve off.

Eve curled her upper lip and shook her head. "Bitch, you making me second guess coming up north to work for you. If you gon' be acting like this, then I don't know." She walked off after bumping Chasity a tad bit.

Chasity turned to me as the speakers started to blare Rae Sremmurd's "Power Glide". She grabbed the back of my neck and pulled me forward so that my lips were against hers. The next thing I knew, I had her ass up against the wall, tonguing her down while she pumped my pipe, running her thumb back and forth over my helmet, driving me insane.

"I can't wait to get up there, Rich. I can't wait until we're doing our thing together." She moaned into my mouth then dropped to the floor and tried to pull my dick out.

I moved her hands out of the way and looked across the room at Paper. He had Heaven's legs wrapped around him, bouncing her on his dick. One of her breasts were hanging out of her gown; the nipple fully engorged. I was tempted to allow his sister to suck me up right there, but then I had to summon the respect that I had for the homey. No matter how cool we were, I would never wanna walk up and catch one of my sisters bossing him up. I felt like we should have more respect for one another than that.

So, I pulled her up and continued to kiss all over her juicy lips. Her eyes were real low and red. Now she really looked like a high ass Ariana Grande to me. Her long hair was all over her shoulders— the edges wavy and cute.

She fell into me. "Rich, let me handle that business for you. I wanna keep you happy, baby." She slurred her words and nearly fell trying to kneel in front of me.

I held her tight, just as Aaliyah came into the living room, sipping on a bottle of Ace of Spades. "What's good with her?" she asked unamused. I could tell that she wasn't feeling the party. Every time I saw her, she was either by herself or turning down a dance from a dude. Though she was fitted in a hot pink Yves Saint Laurent, body-hugging, negligee that did her body justice. I was impressed.

I held Chasity up as her knees buckled again. "I think she just fucked up right now. Come on. Help me get her upstairs so she can lay down for a minute." I put her arm around my shoulder as Aaliyah took the other one and did the same.

Before we left from downstairs, I saw Paper murdering Heaven from the back. He had her holding the arm of the couch while some nigga and another broad fucked right beside them in the same position. That got everybody to going, and before I knew it, a full on orgy had kicked off, though I didn't find out about it until about thirty minutes later.

We got Chasity upstairs and inside of her room where I laid her on the bed. She immediately curled into a ball. "I don't feel so good, Rich. I think that Patron fucking with me," she said through a strained voice. "Ohh, shit, my stomach." She jumped up and ran past me and Aaliyah, into the bathroom where I could hear her purging her guts.

Aaliyah crinkled her nose. "Damn, I'm glad I ain't drink none of that stuff." She shook her head.

I stepped to the door of the bathroom and knocked on it. "Yo, Chasity, you good, ma?" I looked over my shoulder at Aaliyah and she was looking up at the ceiling as if she was over this whole scene already. I knew I had yet to show her any type of attention, so I was hoping Chasity was good, so I could finally see what Aaliyah wanted.

There was more purging on the other side of the door. Then, she started to groan in pain. "Fuck, I'm just a lil' sick, Rich, but I'm good. I'mma get some rest and I'll come down and holler at you later when this shit wears off."

"Aight, but you got all that hair though. You sure you don't want me to hold it back for you while you purge your guts?"

"Aww-a. That's sweet, but I'm good, baby. Thank you for offering though. I'll be okay. I'll see you in a few hours. You bet not fuck with none of my friends either!" She yelled before purging her guts all over again.

I stood there listening at the door when Aaliyah grabbed my hand. She pulled me out of the room and down the hall to the guest room where she was sleeping. Once there, she closed the door behind us, and I sat on the bed.

"I can't take this shit, Rich. I know I said I could, but I can't." She paced with her nostrils flared, breathing hard. "I'm ready to kill that bitch. I don't care if she's Paper's sister or not." She frowned and balled her hands into fists.

I was confused. "Wait, what did she do to you?" I sat on the edge of the bed and looked her over closely. As she walked, her short negligee rose further upon her hips, exposing the globes of that chunky booty. I was trying so hard not to notice but I was high as hell, and she was looking good.

"You, Rich! That bitch really likes you. I can see that shit all in her face, and I ain't going. Fuck that. Then I hear that she's moving up to the city where we are. Oh, hell n'all. Once that pretty bitch comes, I know you gon' forget all about me, so fuck that." She inhaled and blew it out loudly, continuing to pace.

I stood up and blocked her path, trying to pull her into my embrace, but she knocked my hands away. "Damn, it's like that?" I asked, feeling a lil' hurt.

She stopped mid pace and faced me. "N'all, it's not like that, Rich, but I don't know what to do. I fucking love you, and I don't like the way this bitch has been all over you. You screwing her and shit, and you won't even do that with me. I feel so jealous and lost. I don't like being this deep within my emotions. I'm stronger than this. I hate that you knocked so many walls down within me because I don't like being here." She stopped and sat on the bed, hanging her head in defeat, sighing out loud. "I'm sorry, I shouldn't have said nothing."

I walked over and kneeled in front of her. I took her right hand and kissed the back of it, then turned it right side up and placed it on my face. "It's okay, Aaliyah. You ain't did nothing wrong." I looked up and kissed her on the cheek, then rubbed the spot where I'd kissed her. "I love you, girl, and I didn't mean to neglect you for her because it ain't like that. You're my heart, and I'm crazy about you. I just thought we were free to let loose down here, that's all. You know, sow a few oats and keep it moving. No harm, no foul."

She looked down into my eyes then looked off. "Yeah, well I thought that would be cool too, but then my jealous bone kicked in and been kicking me in the ass ever since. Watching all them hoes fawn all over you was killing me, seriously. I felt like they were stabbing me in the heart with a dull knife or something. I hated it." She took a deep breath again and shook her head. "I bet you wish you would have left me back in Milwaukee now, huh?" She slowly allowed for her eyes to look into mine before biting on her fingernails.

I got up and sat beside her on the bed and put my arm around her shoulder, kissing her cheek again. "You good, ma. I don't know why you keep feeling like I'm thinking the worst of you, because I'm not. I love you, and that's that. You're just feeling insecure in your position with me and once again that's my fault, so I'm gon' let you know what it is right now." I faced her and held her chin so she could look into my eyes. "You are my Queen, and you are first. Ain't

97

no reason for you to feel some type of way about none of these females around here because don't none of them hold a candle to you. This shit is temporary."

She smiled weakly. "What about Paper's sister? Are you feeling her?"

I nodded. "Yeah, she bad, I can't deny that. But it ain't nothing like that going down. She about her money, which is why she coming up to the city. She making it seem like she got a thing for me, but it ain't just that. That girl is about her money and she know that I'm eating out there so she trying to jump on board with me before she get there. Game recognize game, and it is what it is. We can both benefit from each other, so why not?" I moved her curly hair out of her face and rubbed her soft cheek.

Aaliyah shook her head. "Man, I got all of that Rich, and that sounds cool, but I'm a female. I see how this girl looks at you. She eats you up with her eyes. Every time you move, she follows you across the room with them. I'm telling you she is obsessed with you. You must not know how fine you really are because you're always downplaying a female's affection for you. But I see it, and I'm not buying that shit." She frowned and laid her head on my shoulder. "What happens if it's more than that? Like what if she really likes you and it's authentic? Can you see yourself really messing with her on that level?"

I kissed her forehead and imagined Chasity in my mind's eye. Like I said before, she was cold, fine as hell and I dug the fact that she was business-minded and all about her cash flow. I couldn't say that I'd never mess with her on a deeper level. At that time I couldn't really see it because I had so much to accomplish.

I shrugged. "I don't know, Aaliyah. Right now, I can't see it, but I don't know what the future holds."

She lowered her head and sighed once again. "That's what I thought. She's way too pretty for any man to not consider it." Aaliyah placed her hand on my knee. "Well, at least you're honest. Just promise me that if ever you guys get together that you won't leave me hanging in the weeds?"

I kissed the side of her forehead. "Once again, I love you, and that will never happen. You are my Queen, and we'll know when it's time for us to settle down and be with each other."

"I just hope it's soon. I love you so much."

Chapter 8

It was Monday. The day that we were set to roll back up north, I'd just finished my plate of food that Chasity had made and was in the bathroom brushing my teeth.

Chasity popped into the doorway with a smile on her face before stepping in and wrapping her arms around my waist from the back. "Ugh. I don't want you to go, Rich. I wish you could stay down here with me until it was time for me to move up there. I'm gon' miss you so much." She poked out her bottom lip and whimpered into my back.

I smiled, finished brushing my teeth and gargled a mouthful of Scope. Then, I turned to face her while the water ran in the sink. I pulled her to me and kissed her juicy lips. "I'mma miss you too, but it's only a few weeks before you get up there. Let me finish handling my business, and by the time you make it there, I should be good. I wanna make sure that you'll have everything that you'll need. I got this. Just trust me." I sucked her lips into my mouth and pushed her back into the wall, picking her up so that her thick thighs wrapped around me.

She moaned into my mouth and closed her eyes. I reached under us, took my pipe and slid it into her, slamming her down on it roughly.

"Huh, uh, uh, uh, uh, uh, uh! Shit, Rich." She whimpered as I fucked her hard.

I had to leave my stamp on that ass. There was no way I was leaving Memphis without hitting that pussy again, and it was good too. She dug her nails into my shoulder blades and licked all over my neck while I gave her as much dick as she could handle.

We finished thirty minutes later on the bathroom floor with me hitting that ass from the back like I was mad at her.

After we got dressed, Chasity wanted me to cruise with her for an hour. She just wanted to roll around the city and spend a little time with me. I was cool with that. Paper was locked inside of Heaven's room, and when I went to tell him what was good, Eve answered the door ass naked, and opened it far enough so I could see inside of it. There was Paper and Heaven on the bed, waiting for her to return to it. So instead of saying anything to him, I just told Eve to tell him I'd be back in about an hour and then we could bounce. Aaliyah waved me off and slammed the guest room's door after I told her what was good. I wanted to explore why she had an attitude but decided against it. I figured it all revolved around her disdain for Paper's sister.

When I stepped out onto the porch, it was so hot that I felt like I'd just walked into an oven. I couldn't breathe, and that was irritating. I frowned and took my shirt all the way off, leaving me nude from the waist up, besides my jewelry of course.

There were women all up and down Chasity's block. It looked as if nothing but women stayed in her neighborhood. They were all outside in their little shorts and tops, either sipping on ice cold lemonade, chilling, or washing their cars. There was a few of them doing that. When I came outside, the sun hit my jewelry hard causing it to glisten in the light. It was like the block was full of gold-diggers because, when I chirped the alarm on my truck, they got to whistling and calling out to me, waving and all types of stuff. I felt like a celebrity or something.

One light skinned female who had been waving at me from across the street placed her baby in a stroller and was on her way over to me, when Chasity came out of the house and broke all of that shit up. "Un, un, Kema, you can stay yo' yellow ass over there. This nigga right here spoken for." She stepped up to me and wrapped her arms around my waist.

Kema held up a middle finger and rolled her child in the other direction, saying something to the other females that were sitting on the porch across the street.

A few minutes later, me and Chasity were sitting under the AC while I cruised around Memphis, taking in the sights of the city.

"I know I done already said thank you, Rich, but I feel like I need to say it again. I appreciate you for stepping up to the plate and holding me down on this business endeavor. I won't let you down; believe me."

I pulled into the parking lot of the lakefront and parked my truck. Even though it was only ten in the morning, it was already packed with women and kids all over the place. I saw a few men as well, but it was hard to focus on them when there was so many strapped sisters running around in all shades and hues, wearing next to nothing. I allowed for Cardi B's "I Adore" to bang out of my speakers.

"It's good, Chasity. I just wanna see you prosper. That's all that matter to me. This dope boy shit don't last forever. I gotta be able to venture off into somethin' else before my time run out, and in my opinion, you're a good investment. We got a lot in common."

I looked out of the windshield and watched a few women set up a barbecue grill. Their children were carrying two coolers that looked as if they were heavy. In the parking space next to mine, two dark skinned, fine ass sistas pulled up in a drop-top, all pink, Bentley, before getting out and walking to the lake in G strings. Both of them were strapped and I couldn't take my eyes away until Chasity pinched my thigh.

"Damn, Rich, if you can't focus when there is just a few females walking around on the bank, then how in the hell are you going to sit beside me and run a strip club?" She rolled her eyes.

I laughed and rubbed the spot where she'd pinched me. "It's my first time down south, and I can't believe how bad y'all are down here. I ain't ever seen so many strapped women in my life. I damn near want to move down here," I said seriously.

I watched one of the dark skinned sistas bend all the way over so she could situate their beach towels. The G string did very little to cover her lower region. She had everything bussed open for the world to see.

"Yeah, well, I'm glad that you're not because I would have to cut one of these broads over you. The women down here play for keeps." She turned my face so that I was looking at her head-on. "I don't want you thinking that I'm some kind of whore, Rich. Don't put me in that category. I honestly really like you, and when I come up there, I'm hoping we can explore each other. I'm not trying to get up there and be fucking with a bunch of dudes. I'd rather go and stay where I'm familiar. I'm a very loyal female, whether you believe that or not."

"Well, I don't mean no disrespect, but wasn't you telling me that the only reason you gave me some pussy is because you just found out that your man getting indicted by the Feds? I mean, don't that sound a lil' bogus to you?"

I wasn't trying to judge her or nothing, especially if she had already waited three years for him, but that didn't really sit well with me. I didn't respect women that fucked off on their men after they got locked up. I found that real ratchet, and I could never respect a woman that got down like that. I didn't say I wouldn't smash her, I said respect her.

"That wasn't the only reason I gave you some, Rich. But in regards to him, he's cheated on me so many times that I lost count. On top of that, I found out two weeks ago that he's been screwing two guards in there where he is, and now one of them is pregnant. After hearing that, on top of the indictment, I just couldn't take it no more, so here I am. I'll love him from a distance, and whatever he needs during his bit, I'll make sure that he has it. The only thing he won't have is my physical presence." She smiled. "I like you, Rich. You're fine as hell, you got these killer hazel eyes, and you're modest. Your body is popping, too." She ran her hand over my abs. "Think we got a chance of being together when I get up there?" She sucked on her bottom lip and looked into my eyes with her light brown ones. She had nose ring that really made her look good, so before I knew what I was saying, I nodded, and she leaned over and kissed my lips.

I was in the middle of tonguing her down when something told me to look into my rear-view mirror. When I did, I saw a black Hummer pull up behind my truck, boxing me in. I broke the kiss with Chasity, just as two big ass red-faced white men got out of it, and walked toward my truck.

I felt my heart skip a beat as I reached under the seat and wrapped my hand around the Mach .11 that I'd gotten from Macho. "Get down, Chasity. It look like it's a hit," I said cocking it back.

The next thing I knew, there was a big as wrestler looking white dude at my driver's window with his body stuffed into a suit that looked two sizes too small. He knocked on the glass with a mug on his face, while his partner appeared on the other side of the truck, outside of Chasity's window. I frowned, ready to buss through the glass. I didn't know who they were, but I wasn't about to let them hurt Chasity or myself. Especially not her though. Fuck that.

"What's good, homey?" I asked after rolling my window down just enough so I could hear him. My hand tightened around the Mach. I felt my heart beating fast and that told me that I was ready to kill something again.

The wrestler looked over his shoulder and pointed at the Hummer. "My boss, Paulie, wants to talk to you. I think it's in your best interest to," he said, adjusting his big shoulders.

I looked into my rear-view mirror and saw my father step out of the Hummer with a black suit on and a red tie. He rolled back the sleeves to reveal his gold cufflinks. They glistened in the sun. People all around were looking the white men over as if they knew they didn't belong there, due to the face that the majority of them were either Black or Hispanic.

I nodded at the big wrestler then turned to Chasity. "Yo, it's good, ma. That's my pops. I want you to roll my truck back to your crib and I'll be there in a minute. Tell Paper I'm with my old man, and he'll know what's good."

A few minutes later, my father embraced me with a hug before we got into the back of his Hummer, and his two wrestlers got into the front as we pulled away, heading to the other side of the lake front. They parked the Hummer and we got out to take a walk. I noticed that this side of the beach was majority white folks, which I guess made sense, seeing that my old man was a Sicilian. He blended right in with them.

He waited until we were about fifty yards away from his henchmen before he came right out with why he'd come. "Look, son, I'm getting a lot of heat from up top about the robbery, and the things that were taken, so we got a problem." He pulled out a cigar and set fire to it. "I need you to knock off a few low-level Italians out in Milwaukee where you are so that it looks as if they set me up to be robbed, and in turn were double-crossed by the thugs they'd crossed the mob for. There is a small family of the Bertolli's that reside on Seventy-Second and National. Don Bertolli will be visiting this family a month from today so he can ask questions personally. During this time, I'm going to be in charge of his security detail. I will make sure that there are a lot of holes in place so that you and your men can come in and slay him, along with the family. During the hit, you guys will have to make sure that your arms are bare so that he can see you're men of color. You'll kill everybody in the house and leave him on his death bed. I'll take care of the rest, and know that these are very strict orders." He took a puff from his cigar and blew the smoke in the air. Then, he scratched the top of his wavy, black, graying hair.

"Pop, why does it matter that we show our skin color? You trying to get his mafia family to kill up a bunch of us or something?" I asked a little bit confused.

He laughed. "It has nothing to do with that, and I'm going to need you to trust me on this." He puffed off of his cigar again. "Son, if I can get this cock sucker out of the way, don't you know what that means for you, and for our family?" He asked with his eyebrows raised.

I looked off into the distance and saw four white girls playing volleyball in the sand. They wore bikini panties and small matching tops. Their skins were heavily tanned, and they kept on making these sex noises every time they went to hit the yellow volleyball. Their big breasts threatened to pop out of their tops.

I looked over to my father who was eyeing them just as hard as I was. "What's with all this family talk all of the sudden. You ain't acted like you cared about your Black family for years, or shit, for as long as I can remember." I eyed the white girls a lil' more closely as we walked past them.

One actually stopped and waved at me. I nodded at her and kept it moving.

My father shrugged. "Yeah, well, maybe you're right, but it's a new day. I'm here now, and I want the best for you and your sisters. If I can get this cock sucker out of the way, it spells millions, Rich. We'll have more money than you could ever spend. This son of a bitch refuses to touch the narcotic side of the industry. Says the bosses back in Sicily forbids it. Because of that, the entire Bertolli family is missing out on millions of dollars. I can't sit back and let that happen. I'm third in line to the throne. Two deaths, and batta bing, your dad's in office and I plan on making more power moves than Donald Trump. I'm going to use you to do it, son." He blew smoke out of his nose and took another pull from his cigar. "That your girl you were rolling with?" he asked, raising an eyebrow. "She's awful pretty. It's gon' take more than a few pennies to keep her happy. Trust me, son. Nice taste though."

I laughed. "N'all, she ain't my girl. Just a good friend for the time being, but I definitely understand what you're saying. Women are expensive, and so am I." I kicked a rock that was in the trail in front of me. "Kesha wants to go off to college, Pops, and I gotta make sure that she's able to go anywhere that she wants. She's a good girl, and she dreams outside of the ghetto. I wish I could do that."

My father smiled. "We had dinner yesterday, and I told her to not tell you about it, so don't be angry. She looks so much like your mother that it scares me." The wind blew his wavy hair and caused the fire to go out on his cigar. He threw it to the ground and kept on walking.

I imagined him having dinner with Kesha and it made me so mad that I felt like punching him in the nose. Especially after he said that he told her to not tell me, and she hadn't. I felt like a bond between her and I had been broken in a sense. Maybe I was overreacting, but my little sister Kesha was my life, and I really didn't want to share her with him.

"I saw that truck you were driving, Rich. It's a signal to the Feds to watch your every move. If you want to be a rich man for a long time, you have to let go of those ghetto ways, because they will only keep you in the ghetto. Rich men don't have to flaunt their wealth so flamboyantly. The more attention you call to yourself, the shorter your life span will be in this game. You're my son, so I want you to go far, and to have a lot." He turned around. "Here. Let's start walking back to the Hummer." He waved at an older white man walking a dog and smiled briefly before his face went back to a frown. "He's a member of the Castellanos. A rough and rugged son of a bitch. You never know who you're around these days, son."

I looked over my shoulder at the older white man, and raised my eyebrows in fascination. I thought it was cool how my father knew him from afar. They'd waved at each other as if they were two ordinary citizens.

"Son, you and I have to bond together and make a way for your sisters. We're the men of this family, and it's our duty to pave the way for them. In time, I would like for you to meet your other siblings on my side of the family. I feel it's time we all came together. Dad's not as young as he used to be." He started to cough and cover his mouth.

By this time, we were walking past the white girls that were playing volleyball. The same one that had waved before jogged over to us and stopped right alongside my father. "Hey, is that your son? Because he's cute," she said, smiling first at my father and then at me. She waved and wiggled her fingers at me.

I laughed. "Yeah, that's my old man. Unfortunately, I'm not from down here. I leave town tonight. Wish I could've met you sooner." I looked her up and down.

The wind blew, causing her long red hair to blow all over her face. She tried her best to get a hold of it but couldn't. "Damn, that's a bummer. I could have shown you a really good time." She shook her head. "How about a hug just for kicks, huh?" She opened her arms with a sexy look on her face.

I walked into them and wrapped my arms around her small frame, noting that she smelled and felt different. I felt like I was doing something wrong. I'd never been with a white girl before, nor had I ever been that close to one. So, it felt weird. After we broke our embrace, I turned her around in a circle, just looking her body over and nodding my approval. She wasn't thick or nothing like that, but for her frame she was straight.

"I guess I'll see you next time I'm down here. Maybe I'll cruise by the volleyball section and bump into you."

She continued to pull her hair away from her face and out of her mouth. "Yeah, you do that. Hopefully I'm here." One of the white girls called her name. She turned to me and waved before jogging back over to them.

My pops laughed as we continued to walk. "Be ready when I reach out to you, Rich. Time is of the essence, and you'll have to do everything just as I command you to. Once I'm in the Don's seat, the sky is the limit."

* * *

I wrapped my arms around Chasity and held her, while we stood out in the street, in front of my open truck door. She stomped her foot and looked up at me with a sad expression on her face. The block had only one street light in the middle of it, so in order to see her clearly, I had to open my truck's door and use the interior light.

"What's the matter, baby?"

"I don't want you to leave, Rich. Can't you just chill here with me for one more night? I mean, I don't mean to be all needy and shit, but, damn. I'mma miss you too bad."

Aaliyah got into the passenger's seat and slammed the door, causing the truck to rock a little bit. I looked over my shoulder at her and she refused to look me in the eyes. Instead she turned up the radio so that my trunk was knocking.

I wanted to say something but didn't. Instead, I looked down at Chasity and kissed her lips. "You'll be up there in less than a month. We both gotta be on business until then. You hold me down, and I'll do the same for you, aiight?" I hugged her tightly, sniffing her up and everything.

She squeezed me back. "You ain't gotta worry about that, Rich. Now that I got a taste of you, I feel like I'm addicted, so I'll handle my end. You just do the same." She stepped on her tippy toes and kissed my lips.

Paper pulled to the side of us, with his truck beating loudly. "Man, y'all break up all that affectionate shit. I don't wanna see that." He laughed, puffing on a fat ass Garcia Vega.

Chasity rolled her eyes. "Well you better get used to it because when I come up there, I'm locking his ass down. I'm letting you know that right now." She laid her head back on my chest.

Paper blew his weed smoke in the air. "Bruh, just a heads up, Heaven coming back with me. Say she can't let a nigga go ever since I beat that shit up." He looked over to her as she sat in his passenger's seat, smoking her own blunt, and laughed loudly.

She moved so that she could say something to stand up for herself. "Girl, you already know what it is. Don't let this nigga jack on my name like that." She pushed Paper playfully.

Paper continued to laugh. "Just letting you know, bruh, and we out." He pulled in front of my truck and they parked.

I hugged Chasity real tight one more time before I climbed into my truck. "I'mma get at you in a few, Lil' One, aiight."

She nodded and took a step back so I could pull away from the curb. "You better hit me up, Rich. I ain't playing."

I nodded. "I will, and you remember everything I said, and stay focused. If it don't make dollas, it don't make sense." Those were the last words I said to her before I pulled off of her block and out of Memphis.

The ride back was extremely quiet, with the exception of the music. Aaliyah barely gave me any wordplay. I could tell that she was heated at me.

Chapter 9

We'd been back in the city for three weeks and hustling harder than ever. Now we had four trap houses that were doing at least eighty bands apiece a day. Because of that, we had to hire more young hustlers, and keep Andrea in the kitchen whipping that work more than ever before. It seemed like every time I'd stop at one trap house to pick up a bag of money, and drop off another kilo, I'd be called to another one to do the same thing. I felt like I was being knocked back and forth for the positive.

It got to the point where Andrea had to sit me down and show me how to mix the cocaine with meth myself because I was having her cook so much of it, for long periods of times. It didn't take long for me to master the whipping game, and before I knew it, I was a pro, and cooking at least a bird a day.

I wanted to show Paper how to whip too, but by this time, the homey was tooting powder real heavy. I don't know what had gotten him to doing it, but he had, and he went through about an ounce a day. I didn't feel like it was a cause for concern at this time.

Because we were slanging so much dope in our area, we started to get famous and known for our hustle. It got to the point that whenever we went into the restaurants around the hood, our orders were free, or they wouldn't take our money, no matter how much we insisted. Paper didn't see no problem with it, but it made me feel some type of way because I felt like we were taking food out of the mouths of people that had worked hard to earn a living. It ate at my conscious, so from time to time I'd send some of the lil' homies into certain places and have them overpay, or leave healthy tips that ranged anywhere from fifty to a thousand dollars.

There was a main landlord that owned most of the properties and establishments in our hood. His name was Jeffrey Dyson. He was a well-dressed, mulatto man with a standoffish type of attitude. That was until I started hitting his hand and pay up a lot of the rents for the businesses in our area. After I started to do that on a regular basis, it got to the point that he was flagging me down, or sending me bottles of champagne whenever we'd run into each other in the clubs. But I wasn't paying the bills for the businesses in our hood just for the sport. N'all. I had a better game plan in mind.

Most referred to it as money laundering, but in the hood we called it turning dirty money clean, and that was just what I needed to do, because the money was coming so fast that I was running out of places to keep it.

One day, as I was coming from having a nice meal at Tonya's Soul Food House, Jeffrey pulled up on me in his Benz truck, rolled down the window and asked me if I had a few minutes so I could speak to him. I nodded, and a few minutes later, I had the person that was going to help me turn our dirty money clean. The conversation was a long one, but was summed up as such.

I got into his passenger's seat and the first thing he said was, "I know you're a busy man, so I'll be as brief as I possibly can." He pulled away from the curb and turned his air conditioner up a little more. "You mind if we take a short ride?"

I looked down at my Rolex and shook my head. "It's good. Let's roll." I sat back in the seat and put my seatbelt around me.

He turned down the Teddy Pendergrass album that he'd been listening to and made a right turn. "Look, I see that you're a businessman, so I wanna run some things by you. I'm not dumb to the game, and it's obvious as to what you're doing. My question to you is, how would you like to wash that dirty money?"

I smiled and sipped from the apple juice in my hand. "What do you propose?" I looked out of the window and saw two heavy-set sistas pushing strollers down the street. They looked as if they were arguing about something.

He shrugged. "For every fifty thousand I cleanse for you, you give me five hundred. That's about five percent." He made another right turn. "Also, I'm looking to get out of the real estate game. Well, at least the one in Wisconsin, and I'm looking for a buyer to take over my properties in the 53206. It's mostly low-rent duplexes, but there are some businesses that are flourishing. The neighborhood is up and coming. With the right guidance, who knows. Maybe this area can be something special." He smiled and rolled down a block where there were about fifteen dudes on it with blue rags covering their faces.

They mugged his Benz and one of them lifted up his shirt to expose the handle of a Tech .9.

I took another sip from my juice. "I'm letting you know right Now, Jeff, I don't play about my money." I curled my upper lip as we turned on to another block.

It seemed as if all of the bangers were out, because as we rolled down this block, I spotted another group of about twenty men with blue rags, grouped up, and mugging the whip as we rolled past them.

Jeffrey shook his head. "I don't play about mine either. I'm merely extending you an olive branch because you can't last long in this game with dirty money. Sooner or later you'll need to have some form of legitimacy, or you'll be in trouble down the road. I ain't new to this shit, lil' brother. I started off just like you— hustling in the hood with no direction— until an old head pulled my coat onto a few things. Now, here I am." He pulled back onto the street that we'd started on, right behind my Audi truck. "I mean, you're your own man. I just thought that since I've heard nothing but good things from the locals in regards to you, that I'd see what you thought."

I took another sip from my apple juice. "I'll give you five percent of all revenue, if you'll let me buy you out of all of the business leases that you have before you go. I want to start there, and then I'll work my way toward the duplexes. But first thing's first. What do you say?"

He ran his fingers along his goatee and looked down into his lap as if he was in deep thought. "Why not buy the businesses flat out? That way you can rent to the renters on your own?" he asked looking up at me.

I nodded. "That's exactly what I'm saying. I'd like to buy the businesses first so I can rent to whomever I choose. But since there are existing leases, I'd buy them from you, and go from there. My end game is to own all of the businesses in my hood."

Jeffrey frowned and sat back in his seat, then laughed. "I hold ten of them, right now. All up and down Twenty-Seventh Street and Twenty-eighth. I value them at five hundred thousand. You get me that in the next ninety days and I'll sign them over to you, and throw in four duplexes as ten grand apiece that were valued at, at least, twenty. Now, you can't beat that."

"And this deal will have nothing to do with the washing of money right?" I asked to just make sure.

He shook his head. "Nall, it's all separate, long as we got an understanding." He extended his hand and I shook it.

That day, I closed that deal with Jeffrey because when it comes to the game, you have to keep in mind that everything is temporary. Nothing in it lasts, unless you venture out into the real world of what is legal. I needed to acquire those businesses so I could have something to fall back on once my drug empire was either stripped away from me, or it fizzled out into something else. At this time, I didn't know what my future held. All I thought about was my sisters and making sure that I had something to leave behind for them whenever life decided to take a nose dive for me. I had to think a head. It was my job to do so.

* * *

Macho and Porky called me and Paper to their trap at nine o'clock that same night, and ushered us into the basement where I noticed the lights were off as I got halfway down the stairs leading to it.

"Yo, what's good with the lights, lil' bruh? You gon' make a muhfucka trip on these steps," I said feeling the hairs stand up all over my body.

I felt like something was wrong, and I didn't like feeling like that because it made me nervous. Macho and Porky were my lil' niggas, but they were nuts. Straight animals and out of their minds. On top of that, they liked to smoke that Sherm shit and drink thick cups of lean. So more often than not, these lil' niggas stayed off of their rockers, even though they managed to keep their crew in check.

Macho laughed. "It's a surprise, bro, just chill. We got this shit. Y'all are the bosses and you're in good hands."

It was so dark that I couldn't see in front of me, though I kept on hearing some kind of rustling sound. That made me raise an eyebrow and place my hand on the handle of my Glock. I just figured that if anything looked out of place when I got down there I was shooting until my clip was empty. I flicked it off safety and got ready to up that muhfucka in a hurry if I had to.

Midway down the stairs I heard a pistol cock back. "I don't know what you lil' niggas on, but I got my gat out. Anything look fishy, I'm murking it. Word is bond," Paper said directly behind me.

Birds of a feather flocked together was the first thing I thought when I heard him do and say what he said, 'cause I was feeling the same way.

Porky laughed, and as we made our way to the bottom of the stairs I heard the sound of a chain being yanked on. The next thing I knew, I saw Porky pulling on the chain that activated the red light bulb. Directly to his right were three dudes. They were bound and gagged with duct tape over their eyes. To the left of Porky, and further away against the wall, were two big black trunks. One was open and I could see it was filled with automatic weapons. Directly in front of Porky were about ten of his men with their shirts off, heavily tatted with him and Macho's face on their skins. These were no doubt killers of the Misfits. Macho and Porky's riders that pledged allegiance to them in blood and murder.

Macho came down the steps, walked over to one of the bound me and smacked his face with an open palm. "This bitch ass nigga right here is the leader of the Center Street Gangsters, and he say that we can't hustle in this hood no more because we're making too much money. Am I quoting this punk correctly, Porky?" he asked, flipping open a switchblade and placing it against the dude's cheek, looking over his shoulder at Porky.

Porky was a young, cocky nigga that reminded me of Fat Joe. He was bald and everything. He walked to another one of the bound dudes and flipped out a switchblade of his own. "Yeah, I think that's the word I got from his baby mother. You know, after I waxed that ass of course. She say the Center Street Gangsters were supposed to hit us up this Saturday, during our picnic at Washington Park. Now you know we can't have that. Know what I mean, Rich?" He looked over to me.

I took a few steps forward until I was standing on the side of Macho, looking into the panicked face of Fax's older brother. His name was Derez and I'd never liked his punk ass because he thought he was the shit, and treated everybody that I'd seen him come in contact with less than sewage. On top of that, I hated his brother, Fax. He'd robbed me and Paper a few summers back and left us in a compromising position. Fax was also responsible for Paper's mother being murdered. I hated his whole bloodline because of that alone.

I yanked the tape off of his mouth and smacked him across the face. *Smack!*

His head turned violently to the side before he spat blood across the concrete wall of the basement. "Arrgh! What the fuck nigga?" He hollered, trying to break out of his binds.

Two of the Misfits stepped forward and held him, but that didn't stop him from trying to break free. I was high as a kite, and because of the red light in the basement, for some reason it made all of this feel as if I was in some kind of a movie, though my anger was all real. I hated this bitch ass nigga.

I grabbed his throat with one hand and placed my Glock's barrel to his forehead. "Bitch, do you know who I am?" I asked through clenched teeth. I felt my temper getting the better of me, so much so that a few beads of sweat appeared on my forehead and my heart was pounding in my chest.

He looked up at me with equal hatred. "You a muthafucking nobody. That's who you is, my nigga. What? I'm supposed to bow down 'cause you got a gun to my forehead?" He sucked his teeth. "Nigga, fuck you. That's on CSG."

I flipped my Glock back on safety, reached backward and brought the gun's handle forward, slamming it into his mouth. *Bam!*

His head jerked backward before he coughed and spat teeth all over his lap. Blood ran out of his gums. "Uh, uh, you muthafucka. You gone pay for this shit. My niggas saw them snatch us up. This shit ain't over. You can kill me, but this shit ain't over." Blood dripped off of his chin.

Macho came back from digging in one of the trunks. He had a .9 millimeter in his hand, screwing a silencer onto the end of it with a big smile on his face. "Rich, this nigga got a safe house with three hunnit bands inside of it. Now, I don't know about you, but I gotta get my hands on that. You know, for me and the Misfits. We planning a trip to Miami in a few weeks, and that lil' paper will be good to have, to make up for what we'll spend down there. So, I gotta get this information out of him, or one of his niggas." He screwed the silencer as far into the barrel as it would go, then stepped beside me. "Excuse me, Boss, let me take a crack at him for a second."

I politely took a step back as he stepped forward and extended the barrel of his gun to Derez's shoulder.

"What's the combination to your safe? We already got muhfuckas at your crib right now, with yo' bitch as the tour guide. All I need is the combination and you can leave this muhfucka with yo' life. But the clock is ticking." He smiled that evil smile, then slowly curled his lip.

Derez frowned. "Fuck you. Bitch nigga, I ain't giving you shit. Live by the gun, die by the gun. I'm a muthafucking—"

Woof! There was a bright light in the basement and it came from Macho's gun. The bullet shot out of it and slammed into Derez's shoulder, knocking a chunk of meat out of it before globs of blood started to come out of it and run down his side.

He started to holler at the top of his lungs before one of Macho's men slapped a piece of tape over his mouth. "Arrgh! Arrgh! Arrgh!"

Then there was a bunch of mumbling.

Macho leaned into his face and started laughing. "Don't let these pretty boy looks fool you, nigga. I'm 'bout my paper. It's levels to this shit. Now you ready to talk, or what? Nod your head if you are." He looked him over closely.

Paper nodded. "Yo, I love these lil' niggas, Rich."

I was too entranced in what was going on to give him a response. I hated this Derez nigga. He looked too much like Fax to me, and that was causing my blood to boil.

Derez had tears coming out of his eyes, yet he refused to nod in any way. Instead, his chest heaved and sweat dripped off of his forehead and along the side of his face.

The basement felt a million degrees hotter, and there was the apparent smell of gunpowder in the air. All of it was intoxicating me. I felt myself getting more and more excited.

Macho ripped the tape from his mouth. "Speak, nigga! Now!"

There was a loud murmuring from his right hand man that sat to Derez's left. He started to rock in his chair, seemingly as if he had something to say.

Porky kicked him dead in the chest, knocking him backward, straddled him and began to pistol whip him. "Bitch, nigga! Can't! You! See! We! Conducting! Business?" He said through pauses as he beat the man again and again.

"Wait, wait, wait, Porky. I think he was trying to tell us somethin', lil' bruh," Paper said, pulling on Porky's arm.

Porky ripped the tape off of the man's mouth and pulled him up by the shirt, until his chair was back in its upright position. "You got somethin' to say, you better say it now." He growled, out of breath.

There were three deep gashes on the man's head with a constant flow of blood pouring out it. "I got the combination, man. Y'all can have it. Just let me go," he said weakly.

"Shut yo' bitch as up, nigga. Damn! Take this shit like a man!" Derez hollered.

I looked over to his right hand man. "You sure you got the combo?" I asked, feeling like I could barely breathe because I was so hyped.

He nodded. "I bought the safe. I'm the one told him the combo. I'll give it to you. All I wanna do is leave with my life." Blood dripped off of his lip.

I shrugged. "Well, we don't need this nigga no more then."

Boom. Boom. Boom. My gun jumped in my hand as the bullets flew from it and knocked Derez backward. The holes filled up his chest, and the last one had crashed into his forehead and exited it out the back of his skull. He slumped forward in the chair, dead, just as Paper's mother had been because of his brother. I couldn't wait to catch Fax.

Macho smiled. "Well, it's over with for that nigga. Call this nigga bitch, get her on the phone and have the homey them pop that safe. Let's see if this nigga gon' tell us the truth. Say, if you do, I'll let you go. This shit wasn't about you. I know you been ready to knock that nigga out of the way anyway. At least that's what my sources tell me."

I continued to look down on Derez with my upper lip curled. Smoke rose into the air from the barrel of my gun. I didn't feel an ounce of remorse for killing him. I'd do it all over again if I had to. I hated him. I knew that I would lose no sleep like I had lost with my other murders. Even after I killed Jamie, it had been hard for me for a few days. But with this one, I felt nothing. I felt like his murder was the appetizer, and Fax's would feel like the main entrée.

Five minutes later and Porky confirmed that the combination was right. As soon as it was confirmed, he had the safe emptied out and Derz's baby mother killed and stuffed inside of it, before they closed it back. It was my first time hearing about something like that, but it wasn't the last. Once my father wound up plugging me heavily into the game, months later, I would see and be a part of some things that made this look like child's play.

After the phone was hung up, Paper took the gun from Macho and killed Derez's right hand man while he begged for his life. Then Macho killed the last one they'd snatched up. Now, this day, I could have sat back and watched Macho and Porky's crew kill these three men, but in my mind it would have made me and Paper look soft, and we couldn't afford for killers to be working under us if they thought we weren't about that life. So, I set a precedent, and so did Paper. Like everything else in life, you had to have a strategy in order to survive in the game.

The trunk of weapons were split so that me and Paper wound up leaving with some heavy artillery. We let them keep all of the three hundred bands, and this night I felt like we grew a little closer to the Misfits.

Chapter 10

I bought Aaliyah her own crib the second week after we got back from Memphis, and paid up the rent for six months. Then, I took her to the car dealership and bought her a 2019 drop top Lexus, and gave her the keys before we went to the furniture store where she was able to fill in the blanks of her home the way that she wanted to. I wound up coming out of damn near sixty gees when it was all said and done, but I didn't care. I just wanted to see her smile again, because ever since we'd gotten back from Memphis, she hadn't.

The following night, after I'd killed Derez, I got to her crib at like nine o'clock. She answered the door with a blunt in her hand and a blank look on her face. Instead of waiting for her to ask me inside, I stepped past her and into the front room.

She closed the door behind her and walked past me without saying a word. She was dressed in some yellow, lace boy short panties that were, as usual, all in her ass crack. I watched her cheeks crash into each other before she looked over her shoulder at me. "I ain't seen you in a few days. You want something to eat? I got some leftover lasagna in here that I made last night. It's triple cheese and got Cajun sausages on one of the layers."

I took my Pelle Pelle off and laid it on the arm of her black leather sofa. "That shit sound good. It's cool. Hook me up a plate." I took my pistol out of my waistband and set it on her glass table.

She disappeared into kitchen, and when she walked inside of it I followed close behind until I was able to wrap her in my arms, and place my chin in the crux of her neck.

"I missed you, lil' mama. Been grinding in these streets, trying to get everything in order." I kissed her neck. It tasted like perfume and a hint of sweat. None the less, I liked it.

Her ass molded into my lap, and as she popped back on her legs she forced my piece to slide into her crack, creating a wedgie for her. "I missed you too, Rich. I was hoping you ain't forgot about me." She leaned her head to the side so I could continue to nibble on her flesh.

I couldn't stop my dick from getting hard. It was something about the pheromones coming off of her body that drove me crazy. I grounded forward into her ass, and the soft cushions of them sucked me in.

She patted my arms so I could let her go. "Let me put something in your stomach. I know you ain't ate nothin' yet."

I released her and she walked to the refrigerator and bent over. I could see the print of her pussy between her legs. It popped out almost immediately. I had to stop peeping her so close or I was about to snatch her lil' ass up. This night I found myself feening for her body. I don't know why I was, but I just was.

She pulled out the leftover lasagna and set it on the stove, then popped back on her legs. "You know Heaven hit me up on Facebook today, saying that Chasity should be up here in three weeks. I ain't gon' even lie, I ain't ready for that shit, Rich." She turned to look at me before walking past me, reaching into the cupboard and coming out of it with a plate. She then cut a nice chunk of lasagna and placed it on there. Afterward, she put it inside of the microwave.

I walked over to her and pulled her into my embrace so that we were facing each other. "So, she coming up here. What that mean?" I asked before kissing her soft lips.

She turned her head to the side and pushed me away. "Get off me, Rich, because you already know what that mean. You got a thing for that bitch and I know its gon' cause you to turn on me in some kind of way. I ain't ready for that." She shook her head and turned her back to me, leaned up against the counter and lowered her head. "Damn, I hate how much I love yo' fine ass. I wish you didn't have that effect on me. This shit is killing me." She exhaled slowly and turned around after the microwave dinged. Then, she took the plate of food out of it and walked into the dining room, setting it on the table with a fork. "What you want to drink?" she asked walking past me.

I had my head lowered, still unable to get over the fact that she'd broken our kiss. I felt offended and honestly a lil' hurt. After all, I cared about Aaliyah in such a way.

I grabbed her arm and pulled her back to me, wrapping my hands around her lower back. "You better stop playing with me, Aaliyah. If I wanna kiss these lips, then that's what I'mma do." I kissed them, and once again she pushed me away, but this time I didn't let her go. I held her firmly, looking into her eyes while she struggled against me. "Yo, I need you right now. I had to take care of some business yesterday and shit ended ugly, and I need you to help me take my mind off of it," I said, brushing her curly hair out of her pretty face.

She gave me a look of concern. "Wait, are you okay?" She looked me up and down while I held her.

"I'm good. I'm a lil' tipsy, but I'm good."

We looked into each other's eyes for a long time before she wiggled out of my embrace. "I don't know what happened, but I hope you're okay, Rich, even though I feel like you're trying to take the conversation away from the fact that Chasity will be up here in a few weeks. I need to know how that's going to fare for me?"

I covered my face with both of my hands. I didn't feel like having that conversation. I just wanted to hold her lil' ass for a lil' while. Aaliyah was like my refuge away from the slums. We'd been through so much together that at times when things got rough, she was the only female that I wanted to be around, just so I could hold her. Even though I didn't feel no remorse for killing Derez, there were three other murders that took place that night that had me feeling some type of way. The main one was that of Derez's baby mother. I'd found out that they had a little girl together. For some reason that got to me.

"Look, Aaliyah, I ain't trying to think that far down the line like that. I just wanna be up under your ass tonight. Is that allowed?" I asked, frustrated.

She blew air through her teeth and shook her head. "Yeah, I guess Rich. What? You wanna eat first, then we can go in my room and lay up?" she asked dryly. "I gotta be honest though. Sooner or later you gone have to answer me about this bitch."

She reached into an ashtray that was sitting on the edge of the table and picked the blunt out of it before setting fire to it. "I'm not about to play second fiddle to none of them hoes. I don't care what she is to Paper. You take yo' ass down there and fuck this bitch on the first night, and here it is going on damn near a year and you ain't fucked me yet. What type of shit is that?" She took two steps toward the kitchen, and turned back around. "Fuck you want to drink, man?"

I continued to rub my hands over my face. I felt my temper getting hotter and hotter. She was pushing my buttons and I was trying my best to not allow her to get to me.

"Did you hear me, Rich? What do you want to drink? Are you deaf or something?"

I don't know how it happened, but the next thing I remembered was me waiting for her to sit her blunt in the ashtray, then I walked up to her lil' ass and slammed her up against the wall. My hands trailed around her until I was cuffing her big booty.

"You want me to fuck you, huh? That's all you care about is this dick, right?" I hollered into her pretty face.

"Get off me, Rich. What's the matter with you?" She asked beating her fists against my chest.

I picked her up, carried her to the back room and fell on the bed with me on top of her. I tore her Fendi blouse down the middle. Her titties spilled out, one at a time. I lowered my head and sucked the right nipple into my mouth, and then the left, while I slid a hand down the front of her panties and on to her bald pussy lips.

"Mmm, get off of me, Rich. Don't do this to me, daddy, please?" She gasped, out of breath, but I noticed she opened her legs wide.

I slipped two fingers into her pussy and began to work them in and out while I sucked hard on her breasts. I'd feened for her body for so long, and now I was unable to hold back my animal urges. I sat up and ripped her panties from her body with two tries. She yelped and raised her ass from the bed, and I was back on top of her, unbuckling my Gucci belt and shimmying my pants below my waist and off of my legs, until I was left in just my boxers.

Aaliyah pushed at my chest and turned her head from side to side as I tried to kiss her. Finally, I held her hands at the sides of her head and bit into her neck before sucking it with intense pressure. Simultaneously, I ground my pipe into her crease. It had worked its way out of my boxer hole and was bumping up against her wet lips.

"Give me this pussy, Aaliyah. I want this shit. I can't hold back no more. I need you, baby." I pulled my boxers down, then held her thighs apart, took my dick head and placed it on her hole.

"No, Rich, please. Not like this. Not like this. Uhhh! Fuck!" She hollered as I plunged deep into her pussy, cocked my back and got to ramming her at full speed. Her pussy was piping hot, wet, and tight as a fist. I felt her walls sucking at me right away, and it encouraged me to fuck her harder. "Uh, uh, uh, uh, fuck me, Rich. Fuck me. You're finally in my pussy, Rich! Yes! I love it! I love you so much!" She screamed.

I forced her into a ball and got to long-stroking that wet pussy. Its juices oozed all around my dick. I could hear the sounds of our middles and it made me even more horny. Her titties bounced on her small frame. Her face was twisted into a mask of passion.

She reached up and ran her hands under my shirt, rubbing all over my abs. "Take this off, Rich. Let me see. Let me see that body. Uhh-a! Shit, daddy! Let me see!" She moaned.

I leaned all the way forward and dipped my dick as far into her as I could, and kept it there while I pulled my shirt over my head, along with my beater and threw them to the floor, before fucking her like my life depended on it.

"Yes, daddy! Yes, daddy! Yes, daddy. Ooo-a, fuck me, fuck me, Rich! harder, harder, oo-a, shit! Harder! I'm coming, Rich, Uhhh-a!" She hollered, and arched her back while her walls vibrated all around my pipe.

I leaned forward and sucked the sweat off of her neck, then bit into it. Squeezing her titties together, I plunged in and out of her at full speed. I felt my body getting ready to tense up. The pussy was so good that I didn't know how much longer I was going to be able to last without cuming deep within her. I pumped faster and faster. My hips slammed into her groin. My dick shot in and out of her while her juices oozed out of her hole. I saw the way her titties bounced and then looked into her pretty face.

I leaned in to kiss her lips, and then I was cuming full force. "Uhhh, shit, Aaliyah!" I moaned, still pumping into her. My cum came out of me in big spurts, crashing into her walls.

She wrapped her legs around me, then pulled me down until our lips were connected, sucking all over each other, while we moaned into each other's mouths.

"You're cuming in me, Rich. You're cuming in me. Unnn!" She moaned as I unloaded deep within her belly.

I flipped on to my back and allowed her to take over the show. She slipped off of my pipe, took it into her small hand and pumped it before sucking her juices off of it. "I love it, Rich. I love this dick. It's mine now. You're mine, daddy. I'm the Queen." She sucked me into her mouth recklessly. Just as I was getting used to her oral game, she slid up my body and back onto my dick, riding me like a jockey. "Un, un, un, un, yeah, un, daddy! Give me. This. Dick. Uhh-a! Yes! You're my daddy, Rich. Mine!" She screamed on me as if I were a pogo stick.

I could hear her pussy squirting, and the springs on the bed were going haywire, squeaking loudly. I closed my eyes, then opened them right back so I could watch her riding me. This woman that I had fallen for. My female best friend. My queen, my oasis. It was something about me being inside of her body that was different than all of the rest. I felt more of an emotional connection, and that was new for me.

Aaliyah placed her hands on my chest and started to ride me so hard and fast that the headboard was slamming into the wall. I felt myself on the brink of cuming again.

I grabbed ahold of her ass and sat up just a little so I could force her to take me even deeper. "Come on, Aaliyah. Fuck me, ma. Be a savage. Fuck daddy!" I hollered through clenched teeth.

"Uhhhh, Richhhhh!" She screamed, then collapsed on my chest while her hips continued to work, and her walls sucked at my dick while she came over and over again, just as I did myself.

Afterward, we lay on our sides while I held her in my arms, kissing on the back of her neck. She had light hairs there that I found so sexy. She scooted back into me, as I rubbed all over her hip. Our sex scents were heavy in the room, but I was weird enough to like that shit. SZA's album played on from her speakers. She'd lit two candles that were giving off the scent of vanilla. It mixed with the room's odors that we'd caused. I felt like I could hold her forever.

"Rich, I know we're just friends and all, but I just wanna let you know that tonight, for me, was amazing. I'd been thirsting for you to do me like you'd done Chasity. I felt jealous of her because you had. Is that crazy?" she asked, trying to look back at me.

My dick was still deep within her womb, so I scooted closer so I could feel her better. She moaned and rolled her ass in a circle, slowly. "Nah, boo, you good. I got a lil' jealous when Paper was fucking you too. I don't know why, but I did." I kissed the back of her neck.

She frowned. "Rich, I didn't want to fuck him, you know that. The only reason I did it is so that y'all would accept me as your Queen. I been wanting it to be me and you since day one. I just didn't think I had a chance, that's all."

I pulled out of her and turned her all the way around until she was facing me. We were nose to nose, looking into each other's eyes— my hazel ones into her brown ones. "Aaliyah, I love you. I mean that shit too." I kissed her soft lips.

She closed her eyes and sucked on my lips, then licked them. "What does that mean though, Rich?" she whispered with her eyes still closed. Then, she opened them and looked into my hazel ones again. Though her breath was a little stale, it was the best scent in the world to me, right then. I kissed her lips and slid my tongue inside of her mouth, feeling hers try and trap mine before I sucked it into my office. I wanted to suck her juices off of it. I wanted more of her to be within me.

"I don't know what that means entirely, Aaliyah. I just know that I'm crazy about you, and I want to take you away from all of this shit. You deserve it all. I gotta grind for you."

She shook her head. "I don't care about the riches, daddy. All I care about is you. I don't want you to ever leave me. I don't ever wanna come second to Chasity. I couldn't handle that." She held my face in her hands and rubbed her nose against mine with her eyes closed, before opening them. "Rich, I know you're out in those streets and it would be foolish of me to think that you'd be able to be faithful to me, so I'd never ask that. All I ask is that you respect me enough to use protection, and that you keep shit real with me. I love you, and I will never forsake you. I've had my experiences, now all I want to do is to be loved by one man. A man that is you, Rich. So, it's good. I know when Chasity comes up here that you have to do what you have to, but keep me first. Keep me as your Queen and I'll stay in my lane until you're ready to settle down and be with that one."

I rubbed the side of her pretty face and smiled. I couldn't believe that I had fallen for her like I had. I mean, I felt all weird and shit, like I would kill a nigga over her in a heartbeat. I felt like she was my one, and whenever I was done fucking around in the streets she would most likely be my wife. I mean, if I lived that long.

"I promise you all them things, ma. I love you too, and no one will ever come before you, other than my sisters, but that's to be expected." I kissed her lips again, then pulled her on top of me and held her possessively.

I wasn't going when it came to her. I knew right then that Aaliyah was my baby, and I needed her in my life. Every man had that one that drove him crazy emotionally. Well, she was my one, and I was gon' ride for her. I couldn't lie and say I didn't have a thing for Chasity, but what I had for Aaliyah was stronger at this time, and touched me more.

I held her for the rest of the night, and then in the morning we took a shower together where we washed each other's body from head to toe, before fucking for three hours straight. By the time I left her house, I'd fallen in love with her, and knew that I wouldn't rest until she had everything that she would ever need in life.

Chapter 11

I was sitting in my truck, typing up this trap house series, when I got a call from Kesha telling me to rush home because there was an emergency. I asked her over and over again what had taken place, but all she kept on saying was that I needed to get home as fast as I can.

How I made it to Andrea's house without getting pulled over is still beyond me. But I made it there safe and sound. Parked the truck, and ran up the stairs, got ready to put my key in the lock when Kesha opened it, and I ran inside.

"What's good?" I asked, looking around in a frenzy.

She closed the door and pointed to the back room. "Go to Andrea's room and tell her to open the door. You gotta see her. She looks horrible." She stepped forward and hugged me, pointing again. "Go."

I kissed her on the forehead, jogged to the back of the house, and tried the knob to Andrea's room, but it was locked, so I beat on the door. "Andrea, open this door. Now, man." I ordered, worried out of my mind.

"N'all, Rich. You're just going to over react and I don't need that right now. I'll be okay. Go back to where you came from."

"Go back to where I came from? What? Man, you better open this door or I'mma smash this muhfucka in. One, two—"

"Okay, okay, Rich, just wait." I heard some rustling around behind the closed door, and then it opened slowly.

My eyes bugged out of my head when I saw the size of Andrea's head. It looked like a full-grown pumpkin. One that was ready to burst. On top of that, one of her eyes were black and her lip was busted and swollen. I grabbed her by the shoulders and looked her over closely. "Man, who did this to you, Andrea?" I felt my heart pounding in my chest. My vision was already starting to get hazy before she even named the culprits.

She took the towel that she'd been holding in her right hand and dabbed at her lip with it, slurping in the spit that threatened to drool out of the corners of her mouth. "Maxwell brought that dude Ken over here, and he was looking for you. He said something about you're interfering with things that don't have nothing to do with you. He asked me where you were and when I told him that I didn't know, he did this to me."

I bit into my bottom lip and looked up at the ceiling, trying to calm myself down. My temper felt like it was set on broil. I could barely think straight. I wanted to kill somebody. I took a deep breath. "You mean to tell me that the nigga Maxwell sat back and let dude do this shit to you, and he ain't try and stop him?"

She nodded. "He looked like he wanted to say something, but he didn't. Before they left, he apologized on Ken's behalf. I didn't deserve this, Rich. I don't got nothin' to do with whatever he got going on with you. Oh, and I found out he got Keyonna out there selling pussy too. Did Kesha tell you that?"

My knees got so weak at hearing that, that I had to hold myself up by the wall, before staggering to Andrea's bed and sitting on the edge of it. I had never been more pissed off in my entire life. I shook my head. "N'all, she ain't tell me that. How y'all find this out?"

Andrea dabbed at the corners of her mouth and winced in pain. "He said that since you took one of his hoes from him, he gon' replace her with a bitch close to you."

I bounced up off of the bed, took my Glock out and cocked it back. "Where that nigga Maxwell stay at? I'm finna nip this shit in the bud right now." I looked down on her.

Andrea shook her head. "It wasn't him Rich, it was Ken. Maxwell ain't have shit to do with what Ken did to me. I promise you," she said, with eyes wide open as if she were in fear of what I was getting ready to do.

I frowned and grabbed her by the shoulders aggressively, shaking her a lil' bit. "Didn't you say he brought that bitch ass nigga over in the first place?" I asked, mugging her.

"Yeah, but he didn't know he was going to do that. I could tell because he—"

I shook her harder. "And that nigga ain't try and stop him from whooping yo' ass did he?"

She looked to her right and saw my gun along her shoulder and seemed to panic. By me holding it and her shoulders, it made the barrel point toward her face. "Rich, you're hurting me, and what if that goes off?" She asked, nodding at my pistol.

"Answer my fucking question, Andrea. Where do this nigga stay at?"

"He stay on Fifty-fifth and Menicke, out in Wauwatosa."

I released her shoulders and looked down at her. "You must be fucking this nigga again. Are you?" I hollered, losing my temper.

I wasn't really mad at her. I was mad at the fact that I had allowed for Ken to live this long and it had come back to haunt me. Had I killed him when Aaliyah had first asked me, I would have never went through this chapter of my life. But you live and you learn.

She nodded with blood leaking from her eye. "Yeah, Rich, and I love him. I always had. I've never stopped you from doing what you wanted to do out in those streets, and I knew I could never force you to be with me and only me because I wasn't worthy of that. So I just stayed with him, but kept things on the low." She lowered her head. "I'm so sorry, Rich. I didn't mean to betray you like that. Are you mad at me?" she asked with tears coming down her cheeks.

I took a deep breath and exhaled. Stepping forward I pulled her into my embrace. "N'all, I ain't mad at you, Andrea. You're good. But I do need you to answer one question?" I took a step back and looked into her battered and bruised face.

She sniffed a line of snot back into her nose and swallowed. "What's that?"

"Look, you already know I don't play about my sisters. And for as long as you have been a part of my life I have never played about you. Now, I'm finna fuck this nigga Maxwell all the way over because he out of order for bringing that bullshit to the spot where we lay our heads. I'm out there in them streets all day and night long; them bitch ass niggas could've hollered at me out there. But now they want to meet me at my residence, that means I gotta take the gloves off and get just as dirty. So, what I need to know is, how are you going to feel about me whacking this nigga?" I zoomed into her eyes real closely because even though Andrea would be quick to tell a lie, she wasn't that good at it. Her eyes always gave her away.

She diverted them away from me. "I mean, that's between y'all. I wouldn't feel one way or the other." She lied, and I could see through that lie a mile away.

I scrunched my face and shook my head. "Damn, Andrea! You love this nigga like that?" I felt irritated because that would limit what all I could do to Maxwell's punk ass. I wanted to kill him, just as I was going to kill Ken.

She shook her head again. "I'm so sorry, Rich. I just can't help how I feel about him. We've just been together for so long. I don't know what to do."

Well, I did.

* * *

I watched Porky take the battering ram, cock it back, and then forward with all of his strength, shattering the front door of Maxwell's house. I ran inside of it with a Tech .9 in my hand, ready to splash anybody that looked to be a threat to us.

The first room we entered had two older niggas sitting on the couch, playing an X-Box. They were just on their way to dropping the remote controllers when I ran in with my arm extended. "Bitch ass niggas, lay it the fuck down. Both of y'all, on the ground right now, or I'm wetting you!"

Paper ran past me with his black mask on and a Glock in each hand. He forced them to the floor as I continued to make my way through the house, opening every door before I headed toward the upstairs bedrooms. I could hear loud music coming from one of them. I didn't know which one, but I was on high alert. When I made it to the top of the stairs, there was a bedroom door to my right. I twisted the doorknob and forced the door inward, ready to hit up anything inside. But there was nothing there.

As I checked inside of that room, Macho ran down the hall and opened the door to another one, and that's when all of the commotion started.

"I got his bitch ass! Come on, bro! He's is here! Nigga, put yo' hands up!" I heard Macho yell.

I came out of the room I was in, checking each room along the way to make sure no one else was inside of the house until I got to where Macho had Maxwell hemmed up against the wall with a Uzi pressed so hard against his temple that blood slid down the side of his face. I came into the room, moved Macho out of the way and punched him straight in the mouth with my left hand, then smacked him with the tech, causing him to fly across the bed that was covered in money. I guess he'd been up there counting his stash.

"What's this about, man? What y'all want from me?" He asked with his hands in the air.

I took my mask off and walked over to him. "Nigga, you got the nerve to bring my enemy to where my sisters lay they head. Do you have any idea what you just done?" I asked through clenched teeth.

His eyes were as big as saucers. "Rich, aw shit. Man, I swear I didn't know he was gone do her like that. He said all he wanted to do was ask her some questions." He scooted all the back on the bed until his back was up against the headboard.

Before I could control myself, I was on top of the bed and on his ass, raining fists into his face again and again. My bones crashed into his meaty face, battering and bruising him, just like Andrea had been beaten. I didn't feel no sympathy for his bitch ass. I fucked him up; had his blood all over the room.

Finally, I dragged him out of the bed and onto the floor, taking my Timberland boot and stepping on his neck with my Tech aimed down at him. "Nigga, where that fool Ken at right now, and don't say you don't know because I know you know?"

He struggled to breathe, so I lifted my foot off of his neck just a little bit so he could answer me. "First and Keefe, right on the corner in a blue and white house. His address is 1201. I ain't got shit to do with that man. You fucked me up for no reason, Rich."

I stood with my Tech aimed down at him for a long time, trying to convince myself that it would be stupid to kill him. That he wasn't worth it. I didn't see this nigga as a threat. In my opinion he was soft and just in the way. But for some reason, Andrea had a weakness for him, and I felt that if I killed him that it would have greatly affected her in horrible way. I didn't want her to have something over my head so severe. I didn't really know where we stood at this time, but for some reason the love she had for dude rubbed me the wrong way. I wasn't jealous, it was nothing like that, it was just a weird feeling I had.

Macho took the bed sheet and tied it into a knot, trapping all of Maxwell's money inside of it. "Bro, since I'm hitting this nigga's stash, you want me to kill him?" he asked, dropping the sheet of money beside Maxwell's head, and aiming his Uzi down on him.

Maxwell covered his head. "Please, Rich. You ain't gotta kill me, man. I won't say shit. I swear I won't. I'll take this loss like a man!" He hollered.

I blew air through my teeth. I couldn't believe this nigga was so soft. I didn't feel right killing somebody so weak. I wished that he'd had an ounce of gangsta within him, then I would've blown his brains out. Since he didn't, I fucked up and let him live.

I shook my head. "It's good, bruh. Let this bitch nigga live to see another day. I know where he work. I know where he live. He fuck up and will never get a second chance. You hear me, nigga?"

"Yes!" Hollered through his arms that were wrapped around his head in a protective manner. "Thank you, Rich. Thank you, man."

Macho looked me over as if I was out of my mind. "What? This nigga seen yo' face and you gon' let him live? Fuck that, bro. Pussies are made to be fucked." He got ready to empty his clip.

I grabbed his hand. "It's good, bruh. Trust me on this one. We gon' give this nigga a G-pass." I looked down on Maxwell and shook my head.

Macho kneeled and forced the barrel of his Uzi into Maxwell's mouth. "Check this out, you bitch nigga. I don't know why my boss want you to live, but I don't. So, if you make any mistakes, I'm gon' kill you with no remorse. You ain't got nowhere to run or nowhere you can hide. I know everywhere you be. Trust me on this. This shit better stay in this room and nowhere else; you got that?"

Maxwell shook his head in a frenzy. "Yeah, I do."

I rolled down my mask and we bounced out of Maxwell's crib, on our way to the east side of town, where Ken supposedly stayed.

Paper sat in the passenger's seat of the black Buick that Macho had stolen, shaking his head. "I don't like what we just did back there, Rich. I feel like we just made a big mistake. When have we ever let another live after running in they shit? When?"

I rolled through the yellow light and kept on strolling with nothing but Ken's murder on my mind. "Bruh, that nigga ain't on shit. Trust me, he ain't about that life. We would've wasted our bullets killing him."

Paper sucked his teeth loudly, grabbing the pink Sprite out of the cup holder. He took a long swallow from it before replacing the top. "We got plenty bullets to burn, and it wasn't just him there. What about them other two niggas? Who's to say they ain't 'bout that life then?"

I was trying my best to remain calm. I was already second-guessing my decision to let Maxwell live. Now that the homey threw two other niggas in the equation, it was causing me to feel sick on the stomach, like I'd made the wrong decision, not only for myself but for my crew as well.

I exhaled and shrugged. "You know what? I don' t know if them niggas are about that life or not, and maybe I should've handled things differently, but what's done is done. Next time, if you feeling like I should make a different move, step in and say what's good. Otherwise, I'm gon' do what I'm feeling in the moment. In my heart, that nigga ain't on shit, so I let him live."

Paper took another swallow from the pink Sprite. "You're a better leader than me, Rich. If it was up to me, I'd murk every nigga that I thought was a threat, and our body count would be way up there. I ain't knocking the move you made. Maybe it was the right one. Either way, I'm riding with you until the end."

I looked over at him and nodded. "It's love, my nigga, and you already know I got you just as well. Ever since the fourth grade. Nah'mean?"

He laughed and took another sip from his Sprite. "I know one thing, we ain't about to let this nigga Ken live. I'm told that he got a few killas rolling with him just like we do, so we can't afford to not go hard on this move."

I increased my speed, looked in my rear-view mirror and saw Macho trailing close behind our car in the stolen black van. He had a mug on his face and looked like he was ready for action. I knew that inside of that van he and Porky were heavily armed and ready for war, along with two members of their Misfits crew. I felt like one of the best moves that me and Paper had ever made was linking up with the Misfits because they were relentless and 'bout that life. They also took a strong liking to me and Paper; what I appreciated.

"So, how you wanna do this shit?" Paper asked, sitting his Uzi on his lap. "What? We just gon' roll up to the nigga crib and get to bussing?" He cocked the Uzi.

I shook my head. "N'all. First, we gotta find out where my lil' sister is, then we can holler at this nigga. I been hitting her phone over and over again, but she ain't answering. I wouldn't be surprised if dude bitch ass ain't took it from her already."

I missed Keyonna so much. I didn't know why I'd let her walk out of the house the day that I did. If I could go back in time I would change a lot of things.

Paper wiped his mouth and curled his upper lip. "I love Keyonna, man. That's my lil' sister just as much as she is yours. This fuck nigga think it's sweet, and ain't shit sweet about her or us, man. We gotta make this nigga pay. Him and whatever army he rolling with." Paper curled his upper lip and looked out of his passenger's window, lost in thought.

His words were enough to rile me up. I wanted to get at that nigga Ken more than ever now. Him and his punk ass son, Kendell. I felt like Kendell had recruited my sister for his father to pimp, just like Aaliyah had said he did. Because of that, he would pay the same price his father paid.

Chapter 12

The Misfits rolled up to Ken's house before me and Paper got there. All I saw when we pulled on his block was them filing out of their van. They were chasing him and two females into his house with their guns out. Ken had left both doors to his pink Mercedes Benz wide open. I drove down the block and parked our stolen car, then me and Paper ran down the alley until we came alongside Ken's gangway and onto his front porch before entering his house.

By the time me and Paper got inside, the Misfits had the entire house laid out on their stomachs in the living room. Porky held a shotgun to the back of Ken's head while Macho and the other two members of the Misfits forced the five females that were present to lay on their stomachs and keep their mouths closed.

I closed the door behind me after looking around outside to see if our intrusion had caused any disruption to the neighborhood. After seeing nothing out of the ordinary, I closed the door and followed Paper inside of the house where the action was.

"I ain't got no money in this muthafucka so you niggas ain't doing nothing but robbing me for practice," Ken said turning his head to the side, laying on his stomach.

I walked up behind him and kicked him with all of my might, right in the nuts. I mean, I kicked him so hard that I stumbled into the wall. I tried to buss his berries.

"Arrrgh!" he groaned in pain before turning on his side and putting his hands between his legs.

The females started to murmur. They sounded like they were worried for their lives. They looked at one another in fear. They were dressed in skimpy panties and see-through tops.

"Bruh, take these females in the other room and tie they ass up. You help me take this nigga to the basement," I said, pointing at Paper. I grabbed a hand full of Ken's perm as Paper helped me to pick him up while he groaned in pain.

"Man, I told y'all ain't no money here. What is this shit about?" he asked, walking with his knees together.

We didn't say a word to him. I waited until we got him into the basement before I swung and broke his nose with one punch. *Bam!*

Ken fell to his knees, holding his nose as blood gushed out of it. "Uhh! Uhh! What the fuck?"

Paper picked him up and slammed him against the wall while I took my mask off. I was face to face with him. "Where the fuck is my sister?"

Paper put the barrel of his gun into Ken's ear. "Nigga, you better answer us correctly or it's gon' be a problem. Where is Keyonna?"

Ken swallowed. "I ain't got her, man. She don't belong to me. That's my son's whore. I think he on the verge of selling her because she's too difficult. That's his business, not mine." He scowled.

"Where is your son at now?" I asked, trying to remain calm. I wanted to knock this nigga's lights out for calling my sister a whore, and for talking about her as if she were cattle, but I knew I had to chill for the time being. His murder would come later.

Ken shrugged. "I don't know. Last I heard, he was supposed to be taking her and a few of his other girls out of town to catch money in Vegas. I think they left this morning some time. I ain't heard from him ever since." He leaned to the side and spat out a glob of blood.

Paper grabbed him by the neck. "Man, fuck this nigga, Rich. Let me blow his shit back for what he did to Andrea." He mugged the shit out of Ken.

I looked at Ken and took a deep breath. "You sure that's all the information you wanna give up, nigga?"

"Man, that's all I know. If I knew anything else, I would tell you. What my son do ain't got shit to do with me. He got his stable and I got mine. We work separately until its convenient for us to work together, and this ain't one of those times, ya' dig me?" Ken swallowed the blood that ran into his mouth.

I laughed. "Aiight. Well, since you ain't got no more value to us, Paper handle yo' business, my nigga."

"Wait, I told you everything I—"

Boom-boom-boom!

The bullets slammed into Ken's face, causing his head to jerk around on his body before he fell to the ground in a bloody mess. Then, Paper stood over him and squeezed his trigger again, sending shots into his chest and stomach; overkilling him.

* * *

That night I paced while me and Aaliyah watched the reporter try and piece together what had taken place on First and Keefe, earlier that day. Reports were saying that it was a home invasion, slash, armed robbery. That the victims were targeted and it was an isolated event. That the public had no cause for concern. They'd found the five girls tied up and Ken's body in the basement. There were also no leads at that time.

I kept on flipping the channel from one broadcaster to the next, paranoid that they would come up with enough details that would land me and my crew behind bars. I thought about Maxwell coming forward and spilling the beans, or one of the niggas that I'd allowed to live when we hit his house up. I also worried about my sister. She wasn't answering her phone, and even though she did her own thing, that wasn't like her to completely shut me out.

Andrea had been blowing up my phone like crazy, and even though I should have, I didn't answer any of her messages. I just didn't feel like her guilt-tripping me for beating the shit out of her man.

Aaliyah walked into the den, came up behind me and placed her hand on my shoulder. "Rich, you need to calm down. Everything is going to be okay." She took the remote out of my hand and turned the television off, then wrapped her arms around my waist. "I love you so much, Rich. Thank you for killing him." She hugged me tighter before looking up at me with her pretty brown eyes.

I hugged her for a minute but still could not stop my mind from wandering all over the place. I was worried about Keyonna. She had yet to reach out to anybody inside of the family and that was so unlike her. More often than not, if she refused to touch basis with me, she'd at least send Kesha a text message here and there. I wished in that moment that I could have taken my sisters and got up out of the hood. I hated worrying about them every second of the day. I just wanted the best for them. In my mind, they deserved the best life that I could possibly provide for them.

Aaliyah sighed and walked away from me, reached on to the table and took a blunt out of the ashtray. "Here, Rich. Maybe you need to smoke a lil' bit so you can ease your mind. You're going to drive yourself crazy worrying about everything, and we can't have that, because you have a bunch of people that are leaning on you for support."

I exhaled loudly and shook my head, hard. I had to snap out of it and get back on my game. If the police was going to get at me, then I would have to make sure that I would be in the best possible position. I took the blunt from Aaliyah and took three strong pulls from it. "You're right, Aaliyah. I gotta get ahold of myself. I'll be good in a minute. Trust me on that."

She smiled. "Oh, I know. I ain't ever met a man like you before. I know you gon' bounce back and get it together. You've been that type ever since I could remember."

I sat down on the couch and pulled her onto my lap, kissing her juicy lips. "I'm glad I got you by my side, lil' mama. Sometimes it gives me strength to just know that you're here. I gotta get things back on track. It's just that seeing all that on the news and having so many loose ends was messing with my brain a lil' bit, but it's good." I leaned forward and sucked her lips into my mouth again, then took a strong pull from the blunt, inhaling it deeply.

"I'm so glad that I will never have to worry about him again. You have no idea what it feels like waking up every morning thinking that somebody is going to kill you within that day. Ken has been a living nightmare of mine ever since I was seventeen-years-old, and my mother forced me to join his stable. So, the fact that you've taken him off of this earth, well, I can never repay you for that." She kissed my lips, then laid her head on my chest, rubbing my arm.

I wanted to tell her that I wasn't the one that had killed Ken, but I didn't see the purpose in putting that murder on Paper, because had he not killed him, I would have. Apart of me felt good that Aaliyah could finally be free from the monster that was Ken. He'd killed her mother and forced her into prostitution when she was only just a girl. In my opinion, niggas like that deserved to be murdered.

I held Aaliyah more firmly and kissed the back of her head as she laid up against me. "Whether you believe it or not, I'll do anything for you, Aaliyah. I love you just that much, and it's like you always said, in the end it's going to be us."

"I love you too, Rich, and I swear that there isn't anything that I wouldn't do for you either. You're the first experience of love that I've ever had in my life. I feel like I can never be without you. I'd rather die first. Do you hear me?" She turned around so that she was looking into my eyes.

"Yeah, boo, I do, and the feeling is mutual."

That night, I stayed over Aaliyah's house and held her all night. I just needed to be up under a person that genuinely loved me, and I didn't feel there was anyone on earth that loved me more than Aaliyah did. It felt good to hold her and to hear her say that she loved me every other minute. It took me out of this world of pain and into an oasis that was her.

* * *

Paper came over early the next morning, beating on the door as if he was out of his mind. When I first heard the loud banging, I thought it was the police, so I jumped up and got dressed. Grabbing my pistol, I was ready to hit it out of the back door, then decided that they may've had that perimeter sealed off as well, and decided against it. Then, I started to panic.

Aaliyah got out of the bed and put her Burberry robe around her naked body. "Damn, daddy, just chill. Let me at least see who's at the front door before you get to freaking out." She scrunched her nose and shook her head.

I wanted to say something slick to her because she was acting like she didn't understand the severity of what I was up against. I had accumulated a list of murders that would have left me behind bars for the rest of my life, so hell yeah, I was on edge, and I was going to be that way until things died down. I was really wishing I'd given the order for my crew to kill Maxwell and his homeboys now. That loose end was fucking with my brain worse than ever.

I cocked my pistol and looked down the long hallway that led to Aaliyah's front door. I waited for her to peek out of the side window so I could see what her body language would be. When she looked over her shoulder and pursed her lips at me, I knew it had to be somebody at the door that wasn't a threat.

She opened the door, and Paper strolled inside in a frenzy. "Where is Rich?" He asked, grabbing her shoulders.

I came down the hallway, just as Aaliyah pointed at me. "What's good, bruh? Why the fuck you ain't text me first?" I asked, frowning. I put my pistol back into the small of my back.

Paper waved me off. "Man, fuck that. We got problems," he said, walking toward me. We shook up and he gave me a half-hug, patting me on the back.

I took a step back and sat in one of Aaliyah's chairs that were at her table, pulling one out for him to do the same.

"Paper, can I get you a glass of orange juice or something?" Aaliyah asked him, walking toward the kitchen.

He shook his head. "N'all, I'm good. Just let me holler at the homey in private." He waved her off dismissingly.

She scrunched her face and rolled her eyes. "Yeah, okay. Rich, I'll be in the room if you need me, baby." She turned and walked down the hall. A few seconds later I heard her bedroom door close.

Paper wiped his mouth. "Nigga, we should have killed Maxwell bitch ass. Some of the Misfits say they saw him coming out of the police station over on Lisbon. That nigga had to be in there snitching on us, bruh. It's only a matter of time before we snatched up and locked up for the rest of our lives. Damn, we should've killed them niggas." He lowered his head and placed a hand on his hip.

I rubbed my face with both of my hands and tried to think clearly. Even though I judged Maxwell for being one of them soft ass niggas, I just couldn't really see him fucking with the police like that. I mean, when it was all said and done, he was in the streets too. The nigga sold dope and all type of shit, so I couldn't see a street nigga going into the police station and volunteering information. It just seemed a lil' off to me. But at the same time, what purpose would he have to be coming out of a police station? I couldn't solve that puzzle either. It felt like my life was a Rubik's Cube.

"Man, what we gon' do? You gon' let us body this nigga now or what?" He sighed and shook his head. "Man, I'm just gon' keep shit real, fuck trying to feel you out. I already had the Misfits snatch him and the other two niggas up. I ain't ever saw him coming out of no police station, but I can't sleep knowing he and them niggas alive, so I had lil' homey snatch them up and put two in each of their foreheads. Macho and Porky cutting them niggas up, and they gon' get rid of the bodies. I hope you ain't salty at me dawg. I'm co-leader of this empire too, and I felt like you handled that lick all wrong so I had to clean that shit up for you. Nah'mean?" He took out a vial of cocaine and poured it onto Aaliyah's table before snorting it up each nostril loudly.

"Bruh, so why the fuck you was gon' try and give me that stupid ass story first? Why not just come at me like a gangsta and let me know what it was? You should have known that I wasn't gon' say too much. All we got is our truths to one another."

Paper picked his head up and pulled on his nose. His eyes were glossy and a little bucked. "Just didn't feel like arguing with you, homey. Sometimes I think your problem is that you got too much of a conscious; where as I ain't got none of that shit. It's money and murder for me. Fuck all niggas that ain't me or you. Them bitches can eat slugs and die slow. All I care about is us. Word is bond." He poured some more cocaine onto the table and tooted that up just as he had before.

I didn't really know what to say because what was done was done in regards to Maxwell. I ain't gon' lie and say that my anxiety wasn't eased at hearing they were dead because it was. I felt like I'd breathed in a gust of fresh air after being in a hot ass attic for days on end.

"Well, what's done is done. But from here on out, just keep shit real with me. If you feeling some type of way, let me know what's good. Don't blow smoke up my ass and tell me what I want to hear. Me and you are brothers, Paper. Always have been." I stood him up and we hugged again.

Aaliyah's bedroom door opened, and she came down the hall holding the phone out to me. "Rich, your sister called me so I could get in touch with you. Some chick named Andrea in the phone, and she don't sound too happy. Here." She extended her arm so I could get the phone.

I pushed her hand away. "Tell shorty I'll be over there in a few hours. I gotta check on the traps first and handle some business."

At least now I know why Andrea was hitting me up all night. She was looking for that nigga Maxwell, and probably fearing the worst, as she should have been.

Aaliyah sighed. "Why you just can't tell her? She already seem like she got a major ass attitude with me, and I don't even know her. I ain't the one to be arguing with jealous females. It ain't my fault she gotta call over here to find you. She need to tighten up her game. That's all there is to it. So, here."

I grabbed the phone. "Look, Andrea, I'll be over there in a lil' while. I got some things I gotta handle, then I'll be there."

"Rich, where is Maxwell? Please tell me that you let that shit go." Her voice was breaking up. It sounded like she'd been crying or something.

Hearing that caused chills to go down my spine. "I don't know, Andrea. I ain't seen that nigga in a long time. But I'll get at you when I see you." I was taken aback.

"Yeah, well you gotta come help your sister move out of my house. I don't want nothing else to do with you, or anybody from your family. I can't believe you did this to me." She whimpered.

"Did what to you, Andrea? And what you mean Kesha gotta leave there? I'm paying all them muhfucking bills and she can stay there for as long as she want to. You better get off that bullshit. Ain't nobody got time for that."

Andrea was quiet for a long time. "You know what, Rich? You're right. She can stay here for as long as she wants to, but I don't want you back in my house. I don't give a fuck if you're paying the bills or not. Never step your foot into my home again, or I'll be forced to step outside of my character. Do you understand what I'm getting at?" I could tell that she was crying.

My mind was completely blown. I couldn't believe that she was switching up on me over a nigga that had been nothing but a thorn in her side. He didn't pay her bills. He never went above and beyond to make sure that she was straight. And he stayed kicking her ass. Whereas, I, on the other hand, always tried to make sure that she didn't have a care in the world. I mean, I wasn't hitting the pussy that often anymore. But the love and respect I'd had for her hadn't died. She was still very special to me.

I shook my head in utter disbelief. "You know what? It's good, Andrea. You ain't gotta worry about me stepping foot back in your crib. It is what it is. Just make sure my sister good until I move her out of there. It ain't gon' take me long to do that. And I'm still gon' handle your bills. Ain't no love lost."

Her response was to hang up the phone.

I blew air through my teeth and lowered my head, shaking it. That whole ordeal blew my mind.

Aaliyah walked up on me and placed her hand on my shoulder. "You already know that she can stay here. It's more than enough room, and I'd love her company. Besides, it'd make me feel as if you're here with me all the time. What do you say, baby?"

164

I grabbed her and kissed her forehead. "Yeah, that sound like a plan. I just gotta run that by Kesha, but I'm sure she'll be cool with it."

Paper walked over and took a sip out of his pink Sprite that he'd had in his coat pocket. "Bruh, I heard damn near everything she said on that phone, and it sound to me like we might have to get rid of that bitch. If she fucking with that nigga Maxwell the long way like that, and it's causing her to talk that slick shit to you, insinuating that she finna call the law, jeopardizing our freedom." He sucked his teeth. "I might have to make another executive decision." He curled his upper lip, then took a long swallow from his Sprite.

Even though I loved Andrea like crazy, and I should've stepped right in and nipped what he was talking about in the bud, all I did was lower my head and remained silent because the homey, once again, was making sense.

Chapter 13

It had been another full week, and neither of us I had heard from Keyonna. By this point I was so worried that I was unable to sleep for days at a time. I stayed up pulling all-nighters in one trap after the next, bagging as much money as I possibly could. Cooking dope and growing our clientele lists of customers. The money was coming in by the piles, but it did very little. I started to lose a bit of weight because I couldn't eat, and on top of that I'd started to drink more than I was accustomed to doing. While that liquor was in my system it seemed to numb the pain in my heart that I had for Keyonna.

Then, on a Tuesday night, Macho showed up at our trap house that was located on Twenty-fifth and Burleigh with a weird look on his face. I opened the door and allowed for him to walk in and he did so rubbing his hands together. I closed the door behind him after looking outside to make sure that no one was following him, and also to see what the scenery looked like. It was just beginning to drizzle outside. The smell of rain was heavy in the air.

After I locked the door, I followed him into the living room where he continued to rub his hands together. "What's good, lil' bruh?" I asked, looking him over closely. I could tell that something wasn't right, but in that moment I couldn't imagine what it could have been.

He exhaled loudly and smacked his hands together. "I'm just gon' come right out and say it. We found that fool Kendell. Followed him from Mitchell International Airport after getting word that he was supposed to be flying back in town yesterday.

Figured I'd get my hands on his bitch ass, recover your sister and then leave this nigga in a vulnerable position so you could do whatever you wanted to do to his bitch ass. But shit ain't go down like that." He slapped his hands together and shook his head as if he wanted to say something but was trying to build up the nerve before he was able to say it to me.

That had me getting nervous. I got to imagining all kinds of negative things involving Keyonna. I didn't like all that suspense. I wanted to know what was going on. "Bruh, fuck all that beating around the bush shit. What's good?"

"Man, we got dude bitch ass bound to a chair back at the Misfits headquarters, and been working on him since last night to find out where your sister was. The information I got, you ain't gon' like it, bro." He shook his head again and blew air out of his mouth, causing his jaws to be puffed out.

I was getting kind of irritated with this stall tactic. I wanted to find out what was good with Keyonna, and it felt like he was taking forever to tell me what it was. My temper got to rising. "Bruh, spit it out! You getting me real heated right now." I muggedhim with mounting rage.

He picked his head up and looked me in the eyes. "That nigga Kendell saying that he ain't got your sister no more. That he sold her to that nigga Fax to settle a debt." He exhaled loudly.

I felt like I was about to pass out at hearing that. Fax was of course mine and Paper's mortal enemy. We'd just killed his brother Derez only about ten or so days prior to me receiving this information from Macho. In my mind, it couldn't have been a coincidence. That fool Fax was on something personal.

* * *

Twenty minutes later and I was standing in front of Kendell, watching the blood course down his neck after coming out of his nose and mouth. Both of his eyes were so puffy and black that they were closed. He was breathing hard with his mouth wide open. His chest heaved and he was leaned to the side as if his ribs were broken. I imagined that they probably were.

I smacked that shit out of him and grabbed a handful of his curly hair. "Is this shit true? Did you sell my sister to that nigga, Fax?" I asked, leaning into his battered face.

"I had to. I didn't have a choice. Fax said that he was taking her out of my stable whether I wanted him to or not. I owed him ten gees for a deal we'd done about two months back, and I had to pay up with her, or he was going to kill me right in front of my mother," Kendell said, before coughing up a bloody loogey.

Paper shook his head. "Man, I'm tired of playing with all of these niggas, Rich. Muhfuckas steady attacking the women in our families like bitches. These niggas scared to face us man to man." He cocked his Glock and walked up on Kendell. He placed the barrel to his head. "Nigga, which one of them trap houses he got my sister in? You can at least tell us that, otherwise you ain't worth the air you're breathing."

Kendell opened his eyes wide, looking from Paper and over to me as if I was going to say something about what Paper was doing. "Look, man, all I know is that he got a little stable of females over on Twenty-third and Center, right in the heart of the Center Street Gangsters Territory. They sell pussy and do little strip shows for Arab gas station and bodega owners in that hood. I don't know if he's added Keyonna to that mix, but I don't see why he wouldn't have. I think the address is like 2486. I've been there a few times, and them niggas are heavily armed all up and down that block. If you'll trust me, I'm sure I can get you in. Just let me hit up my cousin that works under him." He took a deep breath and looked up at Paper, wincing as if he was preparing for him to squeeze the trigger at any time.

Paper looked over at me with a mug on his face. "What you think, Rich? You think we can trust this nigga?" he asked, cocking the hammer. It seemed like the whole room was holding their breaths, waiting in anticipation for the gun to blast.

"Please, man. I swear, you can. All I gotta do is ask my cousin if she's over there. He'll tell me what's good, and I can set up a meeting with him. I been wanting to cop some of that pure heroin they got over there anyway, and he knows that. He's in charge of operations for its distribution. Now that I'm square with Fax, he'll be more susceptible to fucking with me on that dope end. Trust me," Kendell said.

I shook my head. "This a slimy nigga, Paper. All pimps are. This nigga will say anything to wiggle up out of this situation. So to answer your question, hell n'all, I don't trust his bitch ass. Send this fuck nigga on his way, and we'll get at this punk Fax in our own time." I took a step back.

"Noooo!" Kendell jumped out of the seat and tried to make a move to get away, when Paper slapped him across the face with his pistol.

Paper knocked him sideways before he leaned down and placed the barrel of his gun to Kendell's temple, and pulled the trigger twice. *Boom. Boom.*

He fell on to his stomach with a puddle of blood appearing around his face. His eyes were wide open, along with his mouth.

Macho snapped his fingers at two of his crew members. "Y'all take his ass over there to that side of the basement, and chop him up. I'll get the tub ready upstairs for them body parts and get rid of it afterwards. Don't trip, Rich, I got this scene under control." He shook my hand and gave me a half-hug.

I reached into my pocket, counted out ten gees and handed it over to the homey. "This for handling that business, and I got another five if you'll let four of yo' young killas roll through Center Street with me tonight. I need to check that hood and see if my sister over there or not."

I missed Keyonna. I was silently praying that she was okay. I didn't like how Kendell talked about her as if she was nothing more than a baseball card to be traded back and forth.

Porky stepped forward, holding a Uzi with a gold bandana around the handle. "You ain't paying us for that 'cuz we're family now. If them Center Street niggas wanna fuck with our boss' bloodline, then the Misfits are gonna get involved. You represent our livelihood. We're burping because you keep our plates full, so just let us know what you wanna do, and when you wanna do it, and we'll be there with guns loaded and masks pulled down. Ain't that right, Macho?"

Macho nodded. "Ain't nothing but love here for you and Paper. Your beef is ours, so what's good?"

* * *

It was two in the morning, the same night that Paper had knocked off Kendell. I found myself sitting in the passenger's seat of our black Chevy Astro, with a Tech 9 on my lap and a extended fifty round clip slammed into it, ready to kill over Keyonna. I was tired of playing games. I wanted my sister back, and I was ready to kill as many people as I had to in order to get her back.

I had Paper in the driver's seat of the van with an Uzi on his lap, and five of the Misfits in the back of our van, heavily armed with yellow bandanas covering their faces. I didn't know how I was going to use them as of yet, but I knew if it came down to it, they were ready to wet up some shit, and there was nothing more important than that at this time.

Paper pulled up a block away from the address that Kendell had given us, and turned off the headlights. Parking the van along the side street, he threw the gear in park. He looked over at me with an evil mug on his face. "We should've been got that nigga Fax out of the way anyway after that stunt he pulled back in the day. At least now we know that whenever we faced with some beef shit, we gotta handle it right away, and be done with it." He put his mask over his head and rolling it down his face.

I nodded and pulled my mask down. "You're right, bruh. But that's the one thing about the game. The longer you're in it, the more you learn, and we're getting some lessons that we won't soon forget. You can believe that."

Macho pulled up alongside our van. He was rolling a black on black Chevy Caprice classic that had rust spots all over over the door. He rolled his window down, and Paper did the same thing.

"What's good, lil' homey?" I shouted across Paper as we both looked down on Macho.

Macho had a white ski mask rolled up on his forehead. It looked like it was in the process of being pulled down but he hadn't gotten that far yet. "Yo, we just came off of the block. It's looking like they just letting out from having a party. That address is where all of the people were coming out of. Fax's son is out by his car, hugged up with some bitch. Me and Porky about to roll up on his ass and see what's good." He looked over at Porky, and I could see him cock the big shotgun before Macho smiled and rolled down his mask. "Yall stay close and watch how the Misfits get down." He pulled away from our van and then stopped and backed up. "Wait, Rich, why don't you jump in with us? That way, when we get at this nigga, you can go straight in the crib with me and we can make this nigga go in there and get his father. See what I'm saying?"

I nodded. "Yeah, that sound like a plan. Paper, y'all stay close, and be ready to bum rush they shit. Remember, we running into twenty-four eighty six."

I opened the van's passenger's door, and got into the back of Macho and Porky's whip. There was only one other member of their crew back there with me. He had a Mach 90 with an extended clip. When I got in, he gave me an upward nod and lowered his eyes into slits. I returned his nod and cocked my Tech, ready for action.

Less than two minutes later, Porky pulled onto the block that Kendell had given us. There were people everywhere. Most were walking to their cars in twos, staggering as if they were drunk or under the influence. I looked from left to right, sizing up the couples. In my opinion, they looked harmless. Just seemed as if they were leaving a good party and ready to continue the action at another location, or in the privacy of their own homes.

It was pitch black outside. There were two street lights that illuminated the block, but they were flashing on and off. Porky slowly cruised down the block at about five miles an hour.

Macho pointed. "He still right here, Porky. You see him? Right here with that bitch." He took the shotgun and lifted it up just a little bit.

Porky nodded. "Yeah, I see them. I'mma pull right up alongside him. Do your thing, Macho." He laughed and steered the car so that he got closer and closer to the couple, until he was right next to them. Then, he stepped on the brakes.

Macho had his window rolled all the way down. He took his shotgun and slid it out of the window, placing the barrel against the back of Fax's son's head. "Bitch ass nigga, don't move. You do, and I'mma blow yo' muthafucking head off."

The female that was with the teen started to scream.

The Misfit that was in the backseat with me had jumped out and put his gun to her head, grabbing a handful of her hair and throwing her into the car alongside me.

"Aiight, bitch, you played yourself, now shut the fuck up," Porky said, turning around to look at her with a scowl.

She nodded and lowered her head.

Macho jumped out of the whip, and I followed suit. He took the shotgun and put it into Fax's son's ear canal. "Where the fuck is your daddy?" He growled.

Fax's son swallowed and didn't say a word. He scrunched his face and looked away from us.

I kneed him in the stomach, causing him to topple over. He winced in pain, and groaned out loud. "Did you hear what he asked? Where yo' pops at?" I grabbed a handful of his dreads.

"He in the house. Fuck you niggas want anyway?" He hollered so loud that now a few people were looking at us.

When they saw what was taking place, they ran to their cars and peeled away from the curb. A few of the dudes that were on the block ran alongside the gangways and disappeared. Now I was worried. I knew it couldn't be long before they returned.

Paper pulled up and parked in the middle of the block. The Misfits that were inside of our van got out and started to patrol the block with their weapons at their side.

"Well, since yo' old man inside, bitch nigga, you finna take us to him. Come on," Macho said, putting the barrel of the shotgun under his chin and walking him into the yard of the house we were set to bum rush.

I walked close behind him, looking both ways as the lights continued to flash on and off. When we got onto the porch, I could hear the music blaring from the inside. They were banging Cardi B's "Money Moves".

Macho forced him up the steps roughly as the Misfits came and surrounded the house. I climbed the steps and opened the door. It opened right up, and I was met by the sights of a flashing disco light and the strong scent of marijuana. I squinted and walked further into the house while Macho forced Fax's son inside. As I made my way out of the hallway, I entered into a living room that had three dudes sitting on a couch with females on their laps, giving them an erotic lap dance. When they saw me, they tried to jump up, but I aimed my Tech at them as Paper and one of the Misfits ran into the back of the house.

"Don't nobody move, or I'm murking shit," I said through clenched teeth. "Bitches, get on y'all stomachs. Niggas, stay seated." I ordered.

The females jumped off of the men and laid on their stomachs, murmuring to themselves. The dudes held their hands up.

"I'm looking for Fax. Somebody tell me where he at right now, or everybody dies," I said, walking over to the dudes and frisking them, uncovering a hand pistol off of each one. I took the guns and placed them on my hip, then slung the dudes to the floor. "Somebody tell me something."

There was nothing but silence from them, but one of the females spoke up. "Fax upstairs fucking one of the new girls. They just went up there like ten minutes ago. Please don't kill me. We work for him, that's all," she said with tears running down her heavily made up face. She looked like she couldn't have been older than fourteen.

Macho took Fax's son and slung him against the wall, grabbing him around the neck until his mouth opened, then he stuffed the barrel of his gun damn near down his throat. "Rich, go see if she telling the truth. If not, Im knocking this nigga head off. I don't like these niggas, and I wanna kill something anyway." He made Fax's son gag over the barrel.

Another one of the Misfits came and took over the living room. He held his gun on the six people that I had laid out in the living room.

Since I saw that they were secure, I made my way toward the back of the house where the stairwell was located. Just as I got halfway there, I saw Paper coming down them with his forearm wrapped around Fax's throat.

He drug him down the stairs aggressively, then threw him onto the floor. "Here go this bitch ass nigga right here, bruh. You want me to wet his ass?" Paper asked, putting his Timberland boot on to Fax's chest.

Fax was ass naked and looked as if he was so high that he was off his rocker.

Before I could give him my answer, there were a series of gunshots outside. *Boom, boom, boom, boom, boom.*

The windows in front of the house shattered, and then more came, this time in rapid fashion. So many that the walls in the house started to smoke from the bullets slamming into them. The drywall poofed into the air and nearly choked me.

"Paper, take dude bitch ass through the backdoor, and we'll handle this," I said. Then, I ran into one of the bedrooms, opened the window and jumped out of it.

I stood with my back against the side of the house as more gunfire was unleashed, and then very slowly I made my way to the front of the house with my Tech at my side. As I looked out into the middle of the street, I saw a brown Ford Aerostar with its side door opened. Three men stood outside of it, releasing automatic weapons at the house. On the concrete were two of the Misfits. They were shot and unmoving— their guns at their sides and a pool of blood surrounding their bodies.

I ducked down as much as my knees would allow, and slowly made my way closer so I could get a good aim as they allowed for their weapons to fire at the crib. I didn't know if they were shooting at Fax or trying to help him. Either way, some of our men had been hit up, so it was war.

I aimed directly at one of the shooters and pulled my trigger. *Boom, boom, boom, boom, boom, boom.* The Tech jumped in my hand as one of the shooters fell and threw his gun into the air. My bullets slammed into the side of their van and made sparks come from it. I continued to squeeze my trigger, aiming now at the other two.

One saw where the bullets were coming from, aimed and shot at me. *Boom, boom, boom.* The siding of the house exploded into my face and made me jump backward. By the time I gathered myself, the van was screeching away from in front of the house and flying down the street.

I ran down the block toward our van. Once there, I threw open the door and jumped behind the wheel, throwing it into drive before meeting Paper and Fax in the alley, where Fax was stuffed into the van, then I pulled off.

Chapter 14

I took the hot butter knife that I'd held the blow torch to for five minutes straight and placed it on to Fax's cheek. I could hear his flesh sizzle and him screaming under the duct tape at the top of his lungs. Sweat poured down his face, and by this time he had so many burn welts all over his face that he looked like a creature.

I dropped the butter knife and ripped the tape away from his face. "Where is Keyonna?" I asked him for the one hundredth time.

His chest rose and fell while he continued to breathe heavily with his eyes closed. "Nigga, fuck you. I ain't telling you shit. You gon' kill me anyway. You want that bitch, you gon' have to let me go and I'll get her for you." He spat, opening his eyes as blood ran out of his wounds.

I cocked back and punched him straight in the nose, breaking it with one hit. I heard the bone snap, and it did nothing to calm me down. I couldn't believe that after all I'd done to him that Fax was still not opening his mouth. I had never seen anything like that before.

His nose was cocked to the left. Both of his eyes were now puffed up and black. He spat on to the concrete, then sat back in his chair. "That all you got, nigga?"

Paper stepped forward and slammed the barrel of his gun into Fax's son's cheek. "Nigga, you don't tell us where Keyonna is right now, we gon' kill yo' bitch ass son. What's good? Where is our sister?" Paper asked, cocking his .44 Desert Eagle back.

Fax continued to breath hard. Because his nose was broken, the air coming out of his nostrils seemed to squeak as he exhaled. "Nigga, do what you gotta do. I already know we can't both walk out of here. Somebody gotta be the sacrifice, and it ain't gon' be me. Besides, his mama was a hoe. I don't even know if his lil' ass is mine, so fuck him." He spat on to the concrete again and laid back in his chair.

Macho walked over, screwing in his silencer, then extended his gun and popped Fax in the knee. *Whom!*

Fax fell out of the chair and onto his side. Blood gushed out of his knee while he winced in pain. He held it and blood oozed between his fingers and dripped onto the basement's concrete floor. He scrunched his face, then slowly got up and back into the chair. It was a task because his hands were tied behind his back, but somehow, he managed.

He grunted. "You niggas ain't no killas. Paper, you been soft, nigga. You think that just 'cause you fuckin with some hittas now that I'm gon' respect you or this bitch ass nigga right here? Man, you got the game twisted. You niggas betta kill me, or on my mama, its gon' be hell to pay the captain. But wait, if you kill me, then that bitch gon' die too, so what's good? You already killed your own mother, Rich. You wanna be responsible for killing your little sister, too?" he asked before laughing with blood running down his face.

It took everything within me to not put a bullet in his head right there. I couldn't imagine what he'd done to Keyonna to make her feel comfortable enough to tell him such a private thing that happened within our family. I didn't know what was going on with my sister, but I needed to get her back home, quick. She seemed to be losing her mind.

Paper stepped forward and put the barrel of his gun to Fax's cheek, just as Macho did the same. "Yo, let me waste this nigga, bruh. Fuck this chump. We'll still get Keyonna back," Paper said with his eyes lowered.

I exhaled loudly. "Nah, bruh, he the only one know where Keyonna is. If we kill him, then she might get murked, too, and I can't allow that." I bit into my lower lip and mugged Fax. "What's it gon' take to get my sister back, Fax. Let's just squash this shit and keep it moving. Muhfuckas can't make money and be beefing like this no way. You already know that."

Fax coughed and spat on the concrete. "Aw, so now you wanna cut a deal. Ain't that about a bitch?" He leaned forward in his seat and inhaled deeply. He gathered his spit loudly within his throat, then hawked a bloody loogey to the side of him. "Aiight then, this how this is gonna go. Y'all let me call my nigga that got your sister. I tell him what it is, and that y'all gon' be letting me go so he can release her at the same time. You can have one of your men meet up with him to recover her, but y'all gotta let me go at the same time. Once you get your sister back, all of this shit is squashed and we can go on our separate ways. Deal?" he asked, wincing in pain.

Paper took his gun away from Fax's cheek. "I don't trust this bitch ass nigga. I say we kill him and find her on our own, then get back to trapping once we do."

"Yeah, something ain't right, Rich. Plus, this nigga got to pay for his sins. Two of the Misfits were killed because of him. I ain't finna rollover and let that shit ride. That ain't in my blood," Macho said, standing beside me.

My head was spinning so fast that I couldn't think straight. I couldn't let my sister be killed. I figured there would be other ways we could come back and kill Fax after Keyonna was safe and sound. I had to make the right move in this moment, and in my opinion, the plan that Fax had brought up sounded okay to me because it meant that I was going to be able to have a chance at getting Keyonna back, or at least knowing where she was located.

I pulled out my phone and handed it to Fax. "Call yo' nigga and make the deal. You hold up your end and we'll hold up ours," I said, feeling like a loser.

Paper threw his arms into the air and began to shake his head, but I didn't care. I had to get my sister back. I was responsible for her.

"Somebody gotta untie me before I can grab the phone, Rich, and I gotta say, you're a smart man." He laughed as Porky went behind him and cut the duct tape, freeing his hands. Then, he took the phone and dialed a number. He was silent for a minute, and then he cleared his throat. "Eh-hem, yeah, this Fax. What's good, nigga? Yeah, we had a lil' situation after the party, but don't worry about that. You know that lil' light skinned, pretty bitch with the hazel eyes that we just copped?" He was silent. "Yeah, the real thick one. Her name Keyonna. Look, if you don't hear from me in the next ten minutes, you blow that bitch's brains out and get rid of the body. That's an order," he said swiftly before ending the call.

I swiped at the phone to try and get it away from him, but by that time he dropped it to the floor. I picked it up, then back handed him with all of my strength, knocking him out of the chair. "Bitch ass nigga!"

He started laughing like a mental patient. "Now what you gon' do, Rich? Kill me and that bitch die too. Be about that life, nigga. You killed my muthafucking brother, put yo' hands on my son, and yank me out my crib naked. Fuck you. Do what you gon' do!" He hollered, jumping up from the floor.

"Nigga!" Paper stepped over him and popped him twice in the face. *Boom, boom.* "Punk ass nigga!"

"Nooo!" I pushed him out of the way, kneeled, and pulled Fax up by the neck. His blood covered my hands. "Fax? Fax?"

He jerked in my hands with a smile on his face, coughing up a glob of blood before fading away with his eyes rolling into the back of his head.

I shook my own head and lowered it before dropping Fax to the concrete. All hopes of seeing my sister alive ever again fading away.

"We gon' do shit my way from here on out, Rich. You being too soft. That bitch ass nigga wasn't gon' give Keyonna up. We gotta go out there and find her on our own!" He hollered, before wiping his mouth with the back of the hand he was holding the murder weapon with.

I stood up and wiped my bloody hands on my pants, feeling it soak through almost immediately.

Macho stepped forward, grabbed both of Fax's arms and dragged him to the other side of the basement, where he laid him out flat before ordering two members from his crew to handle him.

Fax's son was sitting in his chair quiet as a church mouse with his eyes closed. "Y'all better kill me too or I'mma murder all you niggas. This shit ain't over. Word already out that you killed Derez, Rich. You living on borrowed time, my nigga." He curled his upper lip and smiled.

I picked up the phone and called the number back that Fax had dialed, praying that somebody answered the phone. It rang four times and the other end was answered.

"What the fuck you doing?" Paper hollered.

I held up a hand and mugged the shit out of him, so he waved me off. "Hello?"

"Hello, who is this?"

As soon as I heard the voice I felt like I was going to throw up, because it was clearly Andrea's. "Andrea, where the fuck is Keyonna?" I hollered into the phone.

There was a loud click and then it was dead.

My heart pounded within my chest. My next call was to Kesha. She picked up on the second ring. I could hear the voice of SZA in the background.

"Which Andrea you talking about? I know you ain't talking about our Andrea?" Paper hollered.

I nodded and once again held up a hand. "Kesha! Where are you at?" I asked, feeling like I couldn't breathe.

"I'm on my way to Aaliyah's house. Why are you hollering in my ear?" she asked.

186

"Aiight, that's cool. Look, go to Aaliyah's house and stay away from Andrea. I think she got something to do with Keyonna's disappearance. It's not safe, do you hear me?"

"Rich, you're scaring me, but I hear you. She just texted me about ten minutes ago saying she wanted to meet for dinner. I'm so glad you called me."

"Well dismiss that. Go in Aaliyah's house and stay there until I get there. I love you, baby sis, and I'll see you in a lil' while."

"I love you too, Rich. Hurry there."

I lowered my head and looked around the basement. Nobody seemed to wanna make eye contact with me and I understood why. I felt like the stupidest man in the world.

Paper sucked his teeth. "I knew I should've went over there and killed that bitch. Damn, I gotta start listening to my first mind."

Porky stepped behind Fax's son, placed a plastic bag over his head and pulled it tight, suffocating him until he passed away.

I watched Paper pace, mumbling to himself while I stood with my back against the wall, lost in the sauce. I couldn't wrap my head around the things that I was faced with. Mentally it was too much for me to process.

Me and Paper split ways for the night. I made my way over to Aaliyah's house where I wound up staying up all night after explaining to her and Kesha what was going on. I left out a lot of details regarding who murdered who and stuff like that, but I gave them the overview of the situation that we were faced with. The bottom line was that we had been betrayed by Andrea, and Keyonna's life was on the line.

* * *

My father picked me up at five o'clock the next evening while it was pouring raining outside. I got into the backseat of his limo and closed the door just as the driver pulled away from the front of Aaliyah's house.

The first thing he did before I could even sit back in my seat was hug me tightly. "Son, how have you been? I have missed you." He hit a switch and rolled up the partition.

"Not so good, Pop, but I'll be alright. Do you have everything in place so we can buss this move for you?" I asked, feeling a migraine developing behind my eyes.

"Everything is as it should be. My security team are already in place, ready to take shots from your men. Remember they are to aim only at their midsections. No head shots. There will be three Sicilians present. You are to kill two of them and leave Don Bertolli wounded, but not dead. He has to be left alive for the next part of my plan to bear fruit. Do you understand that?" He asked lit a cigar and puffed it.

I nodded. "I got that, but how will I know which one he is. I've never seen him before."

He reached into his pocket and came out of it with a phone. He diddled around with it for a little while, and then handed it to me. "That's him." He pointed to the screen. "Take a look at all of the pictures. Its ten of them."

I took my time to familiarize myself with the man, then sent the pics over to Paper, Macho and Porky, letting them know to study the man closely. They would accompany me on this mission so it was important that they knew who not to kill. "Aiight, Pops, I got it." I handed him back his phone and exhaled. "So, we handle business in two days, right?"

He smiled and nodded. "That's correct. Remember, son, my ass is on the line here. This has to take place, and it has to go how we've planned it to go. There can't be any revisions to our plot. Your arms must be shown, and the Don must be left badly wounded, but alive in order for the throne to be passed over to me. We do this right, and you'll be a very rich man alongside myself. You'll be connected to King Pins all over the world. Money will be plentiful along with respect. But if we screw this up, we're both dead men, along with our entire families, so be ready and make no mistakes. You'll enter through the cellar where two of my men will be. You'll pop them two times a piece and force your way inside of the house. You have silencers, right?" He took another puff from his cigar.

I nodded. "I got everything I need. Finish."

"After you force your way into the house, you'll be met at the stairwell by another member of my team. You pop him and enter the first-floor landing. The Don and the other two will be seated at a long table in front of a fire place. Don Bertolli will be at the head of the table with two guards behind him that will take a few bullets, and take themselves out of the picture, if you get my drift." He blew his smoke out. "You following me, kid?"

I ran my hand over my face and nodded. "Yeah, after they go down, we kill the other two, wound him and get up out of there, am I correct?"

"Simple as two plus two. You do your part and I'll handle the rest. Remember, it has to go down at the time we've designated, no later, so be on time or else this plan will go to hell, and we'll be under the gun, kid, forever. Got it?"

I did.

* * *

I looked down at my phone as it vibrated with my father's secret message to me coming across the screen. It was time to go, and my heart was pounding in my chest. I tried to find my center. After we hit this lick, our lives would surely change. I tried to stay focused on the positive and not dwell on the fact that so many things could go wrong or the fact that I had not heard from Keyonna in nearly three weeks by this point. I missed my sister so bad. Every time I closed my eyes I saw her face on the back of my eyelids. I wished that I could've held her one more time, or was able to redo the last argument we'd had. I would have taken a completely different route.

Paper rolled his mask down and cocked his Mach .11 before screwing in the silencer. "We hit this lick, and we'll be well off. I can't believe we fucking the mob now. Damn, this shit like a roller coaster." He made sure his silencer was as tight as it could be. He laid his hand on my shoulder. "After this, we need to sit down and talk, Rich. We gotta get an understanding, nah'mean?"

I cocked my Tech and nodded, and looked in my rear-view mirror at Porky and Macho. "Y'all remember to let me shoot Don Bertolli. Paper will handle the other two men at the table, and you two just worry about the ones in the cellar, and the other one that's gon' be at the top of the stairs. No headshots. It's all a set up. Paper, it's gon' be two standing behind the Don. I'll handle them before I handle him. Aiight?"

Macho laughed. "It's good, Boss. We done been over this shit a million times. Let's handle business and get the fuck out of there. Right, Porky?"

Porky rolled down his mask and cocked his Tech. "Right, bro. Let's roll."

They filed out of the truck, slamming the doors. I made sure that my silencer was screwed in as tight as possible one last time before getting ready to jump out, just as my phone buzzed. I don't know why I did it, because usually I wouldn't have. I would have usually ignored my phone when I was in the middle of a mission, but something told me to read the face, so I did.

What I read nearly caused me to pass out. It was a text from Kesha. It read, "Rich, they just found Keyonna's body in the alley on Twenty-Seventh and Burleigh. She's dead."

To be continued...

Submission Guidelines:

Submit the first three chapters of your completed manuscript to ldpsubmissions@gmail.com,

Subject line: Your book's title.

The manuscript must be in a .doc file and sent as an attachment. Document should be in Times New Roman, double spaced and in size 12 font. Also, provide your synopsis and full contact information. If sending multiple submissions, they must each be in a separate email.

Have a story but no way to send it electronically? You can still submit to LDP/Ca$h Presents. Send in the first three chapters, written or typed, of your completed manuscript to:

**LDP: Submissions Dept
Po Box 870494
Mesquite, Tx 75187**

DO NOT send original manuscript. Must be a duplicate.

Provide your synopsis and a cover letter containing your full contact information.

Thanks for considering LDP and Ca$h Presents.

Coming Soon from Lock Down Publications/Ca$h Presents

BOW DOWN TO MY GANGSTA
By **Ca$h & Jamaica**
TORN BETWEEN TWO
By **Coffee**
BLOOD OF A BOSS **IV**
By **Askari**
BRIDE OF A HUSTLA **III**
THE FETTI GIRLS **III**
By **Destiny Skai**
WHEN A GOOD GIRL GOES BAD **II**
By **Adrienne**
LOVE & CHASIN' PAPER **II**
By **Qay Crockett**
THE HEART OF A GANGSTA **II**
By **Jerry Jackson**
LOYAL TO THE GAME **IV**
By **T.J. & Jelissa**
A DOPEBOY'S PRAYER **II**
By **Eddie "Wolf" Lee**
THE BOSS MAN'S DAUGHTERS **III**
By **Aryanna**
TRUE SAVAGE **III**
By **Chris Green**
IF LOVING YOU IS WRONG... **II**
By **Jelissa**
BLOODY COMMAS **II**
By **T.J. Edwards**

Available Now

RESTRAINING ORDER I & II
By **CA$H & Coffee**

LOVE KNOWS NO BOUNDARIES I II & III
By **Coffee**

RAISED AS A GOON I, II & III
By **Ghost**

LAY IT DOWN I & II
LAST OF A DYING BREED
By **Jamaica**

LOYAL TO THE GAME
LOYAL TO THE GAME II
LOYAL TO THE GAME III
By **TJ & Jelissa**

BLOODY COMMAS
By **T.J. Edwards**

IF LOVING HIM IS WRONG…
By **Jelissa**

PUSH IT TO THE LIMIT
By **Bre' Hayes**

BLOOD OF A BOSS I II & III
By **Askari**

THE STREETS BLEED MURDER I, II & III

THE HEART OF A GANGSTA
By **Jerry Jackson**

CUM FOR ME
CUM FOR ME 2
CUM FOR ME 3
An LDP Erotica Collaboration

BRIDE OF A HUSTLA I & II
THE FETTI GIRLS I & II
By **Destiny Skai**

WHEN A GOOD GIRL GOES BAD
By **Adrienne**

A GANGSTER'S REVENGE I II III & IV
THE BOSS MAN'S DAUGHTERS
THE BOSS MAN'S DAUGHTERS II
A SAVAGE LOVE I & II
BAE BELONGS TO ME
A HUSTLER'S DECEIT I, II
By **Aryanna**

A KINGPIN'S AMBITON
A KINGPIN'S AMBITION II
I MURDER FOR THE DOUGH
By **Ambitious**

TRUE SAVAGE
TRUE SAVAGE II
By **Chris Green**

A DOPEBOY'S PRAYER

By **Eddie "Wolf" Lee**

WHAT ABOUT US I & II
NEVER LOVE AGAIN
THUG ADDICTION
By **Kim Kaye**

THE KING CARTEL I, II & III
By **Frank Gresham**

THESE NIGGAS AIN'T LOYAL I, II & III
By **Nikki Tee**

GANGSTA SHYT I II &III
By **CATO**

THE ULTIMATE BETRAYAL
By **Phoenix**

BOSS'N UP I & II
By **Royal Nicole**

I LOVE YOU TO DEATH
By **Destiny J**

I RIDE FOR MY HITTA
I STILL RIDE FOR MY HITTA
By **Misty Holt**

LOVE & CHASIN' PAPER
By **Qay Crockett**

TO DIE IN VAIN

By **ASAD**

A DISTINGUISHED THUG STOLE MY HEART
II
By **Meesha**

ADDICTIED TO THE DRAMA
By **Jamila Mathis**

BROOKLYN HUSTLAZ
By **Boogsy Morina**

BROOKLYN ON LOCK I & II
By **Sonovia**

GANGSTA CITY
By **Teddy Duke**

A DRUG KING AND HIS DIAMOND I & II
A DOPEMAN'S RICHES
By **Nicole Goosby**

TRAPHOUSE KING
By **Hood Rich**

LIPSTICK KILLAH I, II
By **Mimi**

A GANGSTER'S CODE
By **J-Blunt**

WHO SHOT YA
By **Renta**

SHE FELL IN LOVE WITH A REAL
By **Tamara Butler**

BOOKS BY LDP'S CEO, CA$H

TRUST IN NO MAN

TRUST IN NO MAN 2

TRUST IN NO MAN 3

BONDED BY BLOOD

SHORTY GOT A THUG

THUGS CRY

THUGS CRY 2

THUGS CRY 3

TRUST NO BITCH

TRUST NO BITCH 2

TRUST NO BITCH 3TIL MY CASKET DROPS

RESTRAINING ORDER

RESTRAINING ORDER 2

IN LOVE WITH A CONVICT

Coming Soon

BONDED BY BLOOD 2
BOW DOWN TO MY GANGSTA